Runaway Fabergé

AN
ART DETECTIVE
MYSTERY

Mary E. Koppel

For information, email Cozy Cat Press at
cozycatpress@gmail.com
or visit our website at
www.cozycatpress.com

COZY CAT
P R E S S

ISBN: 978-1-952579-22-6

Printed in the United States of America

10 9 8 7 6 5 4 3 2 1

Believe it or not, I started this book almost 15 years ago. I would look at the draft (only a few pages) unsure what I wanted to do with it. Would it become a romantic suspense novel? Would I just delete the book from my computer?

Because of Covid 19, I was forced to cancel a trip to Paris during the summer. I whined to a very wise woman named Judi Iverson-Gilbert about missing my vacation and she suggested that since I like to write stories, that perhaps I could write this story: I could travel to Paris on the pages of my book. So I did!

I want to dedicate this book to everyone who has stayed home and who longs for the time when we will all be together again. I also dedicate this book to Judi Iverson-Gilbert for her encouragement and coaching. I also dedicate this book to my sweet daughter. I also dedicate this book to the City of Paris. I hope you all enjoy the trip!

Chapter 1

I am not boring. Of course, I am hanging out at the museum on my lunch break. Marie pressed her forehead to the cool glass display case. The red rectangular Fabergé box glittered, covered with 90 carats of diamonds. It was nestled between two smaller items: one was a silver cigarette case and the other was an oval green and gold enamel box. She sucked in her breathe and slowly exhaled, the glass fogging. She focused on the red box. The box was elegantly designed, delicately crafted and perfect. It was the exact opposite of Marie, or, the exact opposite of Marie's life, if she were going to be precise.

Two hours earlier, David, her idiot boss, had shouted at her. Unfortunately, he'd caught her reading a fascinating Wikipedia article about 'The Hundreds Year War' instead of correcting and preparing the writing on the budget report for the non-profit's board meeting. Tina and Lisa hovered behind him, scribbling in their yellow pads with matching red talons. Thankfully, he had not walked by earlier when she was looking at job openings on *Craigslist*. While perusing the internet she'd stumbled on the obituary of her high school classmate, Rose Milton. How had she missed that?

One hour earlier, the nurse had called, following up on her yearly checkup: lose fifteen pounds or she was going on medication. Thirty minutes earlier, her divorce papers had arrived. She almost had an anxiety attack right there at her desk. She decided maybe she needed to leave for lunch. Marie thought about asking a co-worker, but her feelings still stung from what she overheard Tina whispering to Lisa about how she was going to slam her head into her desk drawer if she had to listen to one more boring story from Marie. So, boring old Marie headed for the New Orleans Museum of Art.

This might have been the worst day of Marie's life except for this one moment—staring at the small paneled box. She loved the New Orleans Museum of Art and the Fabergé Room, in particular. She had come here a lot the last six months to escape. Marie had purchased a membership after Michael, her official ex-husband, had left her. That might have been one of the better decisions she'd made in the last year. At this moment, she questioned her judgment. Had she ever made a good choice? Heck, had she ever really made any choice that wasn't safe or boring? This day stunk!

Somehow, this time, the room didn't help. She could feel the tears coming, her breath hitching. What was she going to do? She was forty, fat, and now she would probably die alone in a cardboard box. She always wanted to travel, do exciting things, meet interesting people, but the best she could do was visit the museum on her lunch break and read books. Not exactly fireworks.

"I guess we know why the peasants hated the Romanov's." Marie was shocked out of her reverie when she heard the voice, turned so suddenly that she hit her head against the case and found herself looking into dazzling blue eyes. The words belonged to a god!

"Oh my God, that really hurt!" Marie touched her forehead and turned away from the man. She didn't want him to see a growing red bump on her forehead—and the spreading red in her cheeks. He was gorgeous—an English-accented Javier Bardem. He was tall. His skin was brown. His pecs and abs looked hard—rock hard—under a polo shirt and jeans. She wondered if his thighs were that hard too, but then she began to blush even more.

"I did not mean to startle you, miss; are you okay?" She finally turned to face him, a little fearful that her thoughts would be written across her forehead like the red bump. She opened her mouth and nothing came out. She was literally speechless looking into his eyes. He began to smile, revealing straight white teeth. Finally, she got herself together enough to squeak out, "I am fine."

She abruptly turned and headed out the door. She'd had had just about enough humiliation for one day. She walked quickly down the marble stairs towards the front door of the museum. She could hear footsteps behind her. "Wait, you look like you might be hurt. Would you please stop?" Slowing at the bottom of the stairs, she turned toward him, just as her foot slipped off the final step, and she fell backwards. She would have a red bump on the back of her head to match the front, when she woke up, she realized as she faded away.

Chapter 2

Paul looked down at the curvy brunette stretched out on the plaid couch in the Director of Security's office. His own plan could not have worked better. He was going to have to break into the museum twice—once to get into this very office to plant his computer virus and a second time to retrieve a few small items. Thanks to this cute little brunette, he could execute one half of his plan now, while she lay passed out, and the Security guard went to call an ambulance.

He turned to the computer, pulling his eyes away from her face. Her skin looked so soft, with a dusting of light freckles across her nose and cheeks. Her lips were a little large, but he welcomed a woman with full lips. He could almost imagine feeling those lips on his lips, his chest, his… The computer, he needed to concentrate on the computer. He slipped his jump drive in, and heard her stir behind him. He needed to hurry.

He looked at the couch and heard a groan. The woman started to sit up; she was muttering under her breath. He could not help but laugh. It was not often he heard words like those coming out of someone who looked so young and naïve. Her eyes immediately flew to his face. He could see red creeping into her cheeks.

"I'm so sorry you heard that. I don't usually talk like that. My head hurts. Oh, gosh, I'm just rambling on. Where am I?" She sat up completely and looked around the room.

"You tripped on the stairs in the museum, and I think you got a pretty nasty bump on your head, but I think that you will be okay." He could not help smiling at her. He did not know what it was about her, but she just made him laugh. Something about her——perhaps it was her utter clumsiness that made him want to wrap her in his arms. *Where had that thought come from?* he wondered. He'd never known any woman who could make him feel that way, but he had to put the thought out of his mind.

"Well, uh, now that you are okay. Uh, um, I guess I better get going. Nice meeting you..." now he was stammering and clumsy. How strange that anyone could have this effect on a skilled and usually suave thief like Paul, but she did. He needed to get out of that room.

She sat up completely, touched the bump on her head and let out a breath. Finally, she smiled. "My name is Marie Clyde." The woman sniffed and looked around, "Is that lavender? That smells amazing."

"I think it's my shampoo. They sell it in the hotel spa. They call it "Peaceful Lavender Mint," he answered, and immediately rolled his eyes.

"What's your name?" Marie must have missed his dismissive expression.

He usually lied, but he answered: "Paul." Looking in her eyes, he could not bring himself to lie to her. What was going on?

"Thank you for staying with me. I feel really embarrassed.

This has probably been the worst day of my life," she admitted sheepishly.

"Really? What happened?" Paul asked, curious to hear what she might consider her "worst day."

"Well, I'm divorced, fat and almost got fired. Yep, and I think they'll probably ban me from the museum after this embarrassment. Oh, and I'm boring! Apparently reading books and trying to make nice conversation with my two bubble-headed co-workers, Lisa and Tina, about anything other than the *Real Housewives of Diamondhead, Mississippi* is boring." She shook her head and winced. "I think I'm going to crawl back home, hide under my covers, and come out again sometime next year. Like, I said, thank you for staying with me." She stood up and stretched out her hand to shake his hand.

At first, he just looked at her dumbfounded. She really had had a bad day, and it was only lunch time. He took her hand, and then pulled her into an embrace. He kissed her. He was not sure why he did it, but the softness of her lips and the little sigh that escaped her sent electricity through him.

He finally pulled himself back and looked down at her face. Her eyes closed peacefully. Despite a red bump on her forehead, she really was beautiful. He knew then he was really in trouble. He released her from the embrace and darted from the room.

Marie was reeling from being kissed by some sort of sex god. Had she just imagined the kiss? How hard had she hit her head? Did that Adonis actually just lay one on her? She opened her eyes enough to see him hightailing out of the room. She followed, shouting, "Wait a minute, what just happened?" She could see his perfectly shaped backside almost jogging down the hall.

This certainly was a turn in events. She wanted to chase after him, but before she could even move, reality began to return. She felt a wave of dizziness, and she needed to get back to work.

Chapter 3

Marie turned the key in her lock and opened her front door and sighed. Her apartment was an oasis of calm. The space was feminine but not frilly. Cool blues and white dominated the room. A couch on one side of the room was nestled between two white bookshelves——a book left opened on the cushion. The space opened into a kitchen with a small wooden table covered with a light pink stripped table cloth and two chairs. Simple, and elegant, a lot like Marie, if she even realized it.

Marie replayed the day's events in her head. This morning had been a disaster until she'd bumped her head. She couldn't get that kiss out of her mind. That kiss had floated her through the afternoon at the office. What a day!

When Marie had returned to the office, the red mark had faded, but she was still flushed. Tina teetered to her desk on crazy high wedges. While picking her teeth with one long red nail, she commented that Marie looked like she was keeping some juicy secret. Marie just told her that she was trying to figure out where she could buy a bottle of Peaceful Lavender

Mint shampoo. Tina rolled her eyes and walked away, twirling a strand of her bleached blond hair. Somehow Marie wasn't as bothered that Tina thought she was boring.

She immediately kicked off her shoes and rushed to the bathroom. She started the tap in the tub and grabbed a towel, when she heard the pounding on her front door. She turned off the tap and headed to the door. Again, there was pounding.

"Marie, Marie, open the door to meee!" a voice bellowed from the other side. Marie laughed and swung open the door. A slightly taller, slimmer and older version of Marie leaned against the doorway holding up a bottle of champagne and two plastic Mardi Gras cups.

"Now, Lauren, I'm not sure that one can drink fine Champagne in a plastic cup!" The two sisters laughed and Marie invited Lauren in, taking the bottle and inspecting the label.

"Well, we're in luck because that is not a fine bottle of Champagne." The two laughed again and embraced. Marie looked at her beloved big sister. She radiated such joy and fun and somehow always knew when Marie needed encouragement. "Before you ask, I remembered that today or sometime this week the papers were coming. I thought you might need to celebrate!"

"Celebrate a divorce?" Marie was skeptical but she proceeded to open the bottle and pour the bubbly drink.

"Good riddance to bad rubbish?" Lauren lifted her cup and then stopped before it reached her lips. She gently touched the fading red bump on Marie's forehead. "How did you get that? Is it a pimple?"

Marie scowled at her sister and turned to the sofa. "It isn't a pimple!" She flopped down and began sipping her drink. *Yes, definitely cheap champagne.* "I hit my head today at the museum."

Lauren took a sip and raised one eyebrow. "How did that happen?"

Marie proceeded to tell her sister about her day and her chance encounter with Paul, the sex god, at the museum. Lauren laughed at the descriptions. As the two sat on Marie's couch and drank, the stress of the day melted away. Marie studied her sister.

"And what about you, Lauren? Is Robbie enjoying his first semester?" As soon as Marie asked, Lauren furrowed her forehead.

"Well, first of all, it's now Robert," Lauren cleared her throat dramatically, "He's enjoying himself or at least I think he is. He hasn't called or texted or Face-timed in a week, but he's happily posting on Instanta-something. I barely see Lance with his practice. We were supposed to go away this weekend and now he can't because of two surgeries that got scheduled for next week." Lauren was quiet a moment and sighed. "I kind of thought that when I retired early that I would really enjoy all this free time."

Marie reached out and took her sister's hand. "You sound a little lonely." The two looked at each other. Lauren shook her head, "No, it's okay. Hey, tell me more about this hot guy! He sounds dreamy." The two giggled.

"Uh, definitely gorgeous and he smelled amazing. His shampoo was called "Peaceful Lavender Mint." Marie stopped for a moment, "You know, I should look that up. He said he got it at his hotel spa."

"Why would you do that? Who cares? You won't see him again." Lauren poured more champagne in the Mardi Gras cup.

"Maybe if I find his hotel, I'll see him there." Marie said while attempting to strike a vixen look and sloshing her champagne on her couch.

"And then what?" Lauren laughed.

"And maybe he and I will meet and talk and fly off to Paris and fall in love!" Marie replied with indignation.

Lauren stifled her laugh, "I wasn't trying to offend you, Marie, but I'm just saying that you would never do that." She patted her sister on the arm, but Marie pulled back.

"Because I'm boring?" Marie asked. The disappointments from earlier in the day rose in her chest. She stood up and went to the kitchen for a dishcloth.

"No, because you're reliable and cautious almost to a fault. That's a good thing." Lauren tried to placate her sister. Marie looked at her sister from her kitchen. She flipped open her laptop on the counter top and opened the search engine, typing in the name of the shampoo.

"Oh, really?" Marie read the name of the local luxury hotel to her sister.

"What about the Ritz Carlton?" Lauren asked, perplexed. She wandered into the kitchen and leaned over her sister.

"That's the only place where they sell this shampoo in the city of New Orleans. Ah-ha!" Marie shouted triumphantly. Lauren opened the refrigerator and inspected the contents. Disappointed with what she discovered, she returned to her spot next to Marie. Again, she peered down at the computer and then leaned against the counter.

"So, now what?" Lauren blinked her eyes at her younger sister.

Marie was about to come back with a brave retort, but she stopped herself. What difference did it make that she knew where this mystery man was? Marie knew she would never go there, even just to see. That was dangerous and she was boring.

"You know, maybe you should take a trip somewhere, Marie,

or take a class?"

"Who would I go with on a trip? I'd love to go somewhere, but by myself? Who would I share it with? Would you want to go too?" Marie asked.

Lauren shrugged and thought for a moment, "Maybe I'd go, but you could go by yourself, for yourself." Lauren raised her Mardi Gras cup to Marie in a toast. Marie thought about Lauren's words and squinted at her sister.

"Would you go on a trip by yourself?" Marie sipped her champagne and watched her sister's response over the rim of her cup. Lauren almost spit out her champagne.

"Oh heavens no, I couldn't do that. You either have to be really sad or very strong. Besides, I have a very busy life." The two burst into laughter at Lauren's response.

Marie put her cup on the table beside her. "Did you hear that Rose Milton died? We weren't close or anything, but I'm shocked. We are, I mean, were the same age." Marie looked to her older sister to offer some comfort.

"I saw that the other day. I remember her. She was sweet. She never really beat her addictions. I heard that she died of liver damage." Lauren slumped into the couch. "That worries me about Robbie. What if he gets involved with some bad folks and starts using drugs? She'd started down that road during college, right after she'd returned from abroad." Marie and Lauren both nodded solemnly. Marie vaguely remembered the scandal surrounding Rose's return from England and first trip to what would be twenty years of entering and leaving rehab. Lauren sat straighter and turned to her sister, "Life is short, Marie. Maybe going on a trip would be really good."

Marie wrinkled her brow. "Are you really worried about Robbie using drugs? Has he given you any indication that he's using them?"

Lauren pressed her lips together, her gaze became unfocused as she thought about the question. "I am worried, but I know he isn't using drugs. Of course, how would I know?"

"You need to speak with him. Tell him that you worry about him. Ask what he's doing." Marie leaned towards her sister. She reached out her hand and patted Lauren's hand. She was going to reassure her sister that Robbie would be okay, but Lauren interrupted her train of thought.

"I really think that you should travel or go on a trip." Lauren offered the advice to Marie. The sudden shift in subject caught Marie off guard. Lauren was not interested in speaking any more about her worries, Marie realized. Frankly, she was kind of happy to put the somber thoughts aside, but she made a note to herself that she'd speak with Lauren about this more seriously when the two weren't already three sheets to the wind.

Happily changing the subject, Marie asked: "Where should I go?" Lauren shrugged and looked around the room, her eye catching the title of one of Marie's romance novels. Lauren walked over and picked it up.

"You should go to Paris. I think that random kiss you got today is a sign. Embrace life, explore!" Lauren was gesturing broadly. Marie almost had to duck to avoid Lauren flinging out her arms.

"You sound like a travel brochure." Marie giggled.

"I sound like I'm drunk!" Lauren tumbled back on the couch and retrieved her cup of champagne. "Let's order Chinese!"

Chapter 4

At 10:30, after polishing off a Chinese food feast fit for a dozen, Lauren's Uber arrived and the two sisters embraced at Marie's doorway. Lauren laughed, but a shadow fell across her face, "Marie, I know you are going through a lot, but I think this could be an opportunity for you, figure out what you really want and who you really are. You should go on a trip!" With that proclamation, Marie shut the door.

Marie slipped on her pajamas and crawled into bed. She read for a little while, diving into the story of a sexy reporter discovering corruption, a handsome detective rushing to the rescue, and their happily ever after.

She sighed as she finished the novel. It was exciting and romantic, but a snarky voice in her head asked: could that be real? Maybe for some bold blond who only weighed 120 pounds, but not for Marie. Her eyelids felt heavy as she turned off her bedside light.

She pulled the sheet under her chin. Despite her tiredness, her mind wandered to the events of the day. She turned on her side and reached out and patted the empty pillow beside her. The tears that had threatened to spill earlier dripped down the side of her face onto her pillow. She wiped them away.

It wasn't that she was all that sad about her divorce, more disappointed. She and Michael had seemed like a perfect pair. They both enjoyed attending festivals, going to movies and out to eat. They could talk about books, ideas and history, but they never talked about the really important things until they did, and when they did, they realized that they didn't want the same things. Of course, that was the big question: what did Marie want? And the questions to follow up: was she willing to go after it? Or was she afraid?

Marie pressed her eyes shut, willing herself to sleep. The question lingered: was she afraid? She sighed and jutted out her chin. She was afraid, but was she going to let that stop her from figuring out what she wanted? Marie felt confused as sleep overtook her.

The champagne must have been really cheap because Marie was nursing a slight headache that had nestled on her right temple the next morning. The coffee wasn't really helping either and there was something else. She turned the conversation with her sister over in her head. Did she really avoid risk? Was she always playing it safe, examining the world from the safety of her desk or her couch, reading about life? Was she afraid?

Marie was yanked from her thoughts by a smell. When she'd arrived at the office an hour ago, she had only noticed a mild odor, but now it had grown worse. Marie turned around at her desk, looking down in the garbage can under her desk. The scent assaulted her nostrils. Could someone have actually cooked tuna fish in the staff microwave? It was way worse than that.

She heard a commotion and shouting coming from down the corridor. Tina was shrieking. Marie watched Tina fly past her in leopard print on her stilettos, all the while screaming. What was going on? Then she heard what Tina was shouting: "Rats!"

Sure enough, four huge sewer rats ran down the same corridor, perhaps following Tina. Marie pulled her feet to her seat and switched off the computer. Perhaps today was the day to work from home? She could hear her manager David's booming voice: "Hey, folks, why don't we all head outside now?"

Two minutes later, the whole office was outside. Tina was sobbing into some intern's arms and then turning to whisper to Lisa who was filing her nails the whole time. The rest of the workers milled about. David waved the group to come closer to him.

David cleared his voice. He wrinkled his brow and affected an expression of fatherly wisdom: "Listen, gang, I've just called maintenance about this. Looks like we have an infestation…"

"An infestation, oh my God, we're all going to die!" Tina wailed. Marie pressed her lips together trying not laugh at the spectacle. Today was already going better than yesterday.

"As I was saying, we may have an infestation, so the exterminators have been called…" David tried to continue, but Tina grabbed the sleeve of David's blazer.

"Oh thank God! Does anyone have poison on them? Marie, what about you?" Tina swung around in her hysterics and fixed her eyes on Marie. "You know all about these kind of things, right? You read stuff? What do we do? Rats have diseases, like plague or something." Marie pressed her lips together and looked heavenward.

"Uh, well, Tina, you're right, rats carry diseases." Marie knew it was wrong to encourage Tina in her freak out, but she couldn't help herself. Tina nervously chewed on her thumb nail. David shot daggers at Marie with his eyes. "But I think the best thing to do right now would be to listen to what David has to say," Marie smiled nervously. This was getting ridiculous.

"As I was saying," David practically growled out, "the exterminators have been called, but they can't get her until Friday. I suggest that we all collect our personal items and work from home..." He tried to detach Tina from his sleeve, but her red nails dug into the coat. "If you'd all just..." again David was interrupted, but this time is was by a piercing alarm and flashing lights coming from inside the building. The sprinkler system went off. David looked through the front doors in horror. Marie slapped her hand over her mouth, lest anyone hear the peals of laughter that were about to erupt from her.

Marie swung around and started walking from the building towards her car in the parking lot. Behind her, her co-workers and all the other people who were in offices on their floor erupted in howls. She pulled her phone from her purse and dialed Lauren's number. She waited for her sister to pick up and then the laugh exploded.

"Lauren, you will not believe what just happened." Marie had to lean on her car, she was laughing so hard. She breathed in and out, but the giggles kept coming.

"Marie, what in the world has gotten into you?" Lauren asked.

Marie cleared her throat, "I have the rest of the day off. Meet me at the museum. Let's see if we can find my mystery man!"

"Ooh, I'm game. More importantly, we can grab beignets in City Park." Lauren hung up and Marie hopped into her car, driving away as a firetruck pulled up to the building.

Marie arrived at the museum in fifteen minutes, finding a spot out front. Her sister pulled up behind her.

"So, how did you get the day off? You didn't get fired, did you?" Lauren grabbed her sister's arm. Marie shook her head. The two walked around the circular fountain at the front of the museum and quickly ran up the steps.

"I wouldn't have been laughing if that had happened. No, we had some sort of crazy rat infestation and the fire alarm went off and the sprinklers too." Marie chuckled as she thought about Tina's histrionics. She wiped a small tear from the corner of her eye. Lauren looked at Marie with wide eyes and a smile crept across her face.

The two entered the museum. Marie gave her pass to the distracted woman behind the membership counter. The woman gestured toward the register book where visitors were invited to write down their names and addresses. Marie shook her head no, but Lauren scribbled in her name and address.

"Okay, where should we go first? Impressionists?" Lauren looked to her left and right. "Perhaps we should swing by the modern art gallery and then grab some doughnuts?"

"Shhh, Lauren, don't you want to see where I met my mystery man?" Marie whispered.

"Oh, of course, of course, lead on," Lauren answered dramatically. They both giggled again.

The two took the marble steps in front of them quickly, turning to the right and heading toward the room housing the Fabergé items. Before they could get closer, a policeman blocked their path.

"What's going on?" Lauren tried to look behind the officer blocking the Fabergé room. Two men exited the room—a patrol man and a tall man in a suit. The tall man slowly turned around in a circle, his eyes peering at the ceiling. Marie followed the trail of his eyes, puzzling at what he was looking for. When she looked back down, his laser focus was on her.

The man pushed past the two policemen and stood, looming over Marie and Lauren. "May I help you ladies?" he asked, his piercing grey eyes boring a hole into Marie's forehead.

"We wanted to see the Fabergé," Lauren answered the man in a whisper. The man raised one eyebrow.

"Really? Have you been here before? Perhaps, yesterday?" The man glared at Marie. Both women gulped. This guy was intense.

"I was here yesterday," Marie answered the man, finally finding her voice.

"I see." The man leaned down, hulking over Marie, "Yesterday there was a break-in here, in this room, and something was stolen." He straightened up and resumed his stare, waiting for Marie's response.

"Really? Wow. What was stolen? Do you know who did it? Was it some international ring of thieves?" Marie blurted out before she could stop herself. Whatever intimidation she felt before totally evaporated. She was curious. The tall man's expression transformed from menacing to annoyed.

"This is an ongoing investigation and I'm not at liberty to discuss what was stolen or who we suspect." Once again, he set his face in a Clint-Eastwood-like firmness. "When you were here yesterday, did you see anyone else in the room? Or perhaps you're a member of an international ring of thieves?"

Marie was not quite sure if he was joking. She stood quiet until Lauren piped up, "I beg your pardon, sir. You're speaking to my sister and she is not a member of an international ring of thieves. She's not that exciting." Lauren placed her hands on her hips and took one step toward the tall man. The man drew a long breath through his nose and looked up. Marie elbowed her sister.

"Madame, would you mind giving me your name?" the man

asked Marie who nodded.

"My name is Marie Clyde." The man pulled a small notebook from his pocket and began to scribble something down. Marie leaned forward to try to see what he was writing, but he held the notebook closer to his chest.

"Is that Clyde like Bonnie and Clyde?" the man asked, raising an eyebrow. Marie thought about the question until she realized that he was making a stupid joke.

"Are you hitting on my sister?" asked Lauren, "because she's divorced." She took a step towards the tall man. His eyes immediately widened and he shook his head. Marie looked aghast at her sister.

"May I please have your phone number, Ms. Clyde," he continued, "because we may need to contact you about your visit to the museum yesterday. That's all. You can give it to Officer Davis here." The man spoke stiffly and uncomfortably and then he pivoted from the two women and walked away. A police officer who was behind the tall man gave a sheepish smile and wrote down Marie's number.

Marie watched the tall man walk back toward the Fabergé room. Despite being so lean, he looked solid. There were probably muscles under that fancy grey suit that one didn't get from the gym—perhaps from eating broken glass? Marie laughed to herself at her thought. The man stopped to talk to a familiar-looking snow-haired woman in a black silk suit with a bright ruby pin on her lapel. It appeared that the two were arguing when another man approached them. He stood behind the woman, looking like a retired line-backer with his broken nose and old brown suit.

Marie nudged her sister as the two turned around to head to another section of the museum. "Did that lady look kind of familiar to you?"

"Which lady?" Lauren looked side to side, then her eyes spotted the older woman Marie was looking at. Lauren released a sigh, "Oh, her. Of course, that's Lydia Milton; she's a huge patron of the museum." Marie nodded. "But there's something else," Lauren whispered, "She's Rose's mother."

Marie felt pity for the woman. She turned back toward the woman. The older woman was now carefully making her way down the marble stairs in the center of the New Orleans Museum of Art. Marie trotted down the steps quickly, smiling to herself as she remembered herself tumbling to the bottom of the staircase the day before. She followed Mrs. Milton and the enormous gentleman in the brown suit as they walked to the front desk of the museum.

"Mrs. Milton, excuse me, Mrs. Milton." Marie reached out to tap the woman on her shoulder, but the man in the brown suit immediately swung around and stepped between Marie and the woman like a wall of muscles.

"May I help you?" The man glowered at her through bushy brown eyebrows. The man looked like a boxer. Marie pulled back her hand, afraid that he would grab it and rip it off.

The elegant older woman turned around to see who was behind her. Mrs. Milton was striking with glossy white hair pulled into a tight bun and an unlined face. "Hank, please." She gently patted the giant's arm and his face seemed to soften. She smiled broadly, revealing perfectly straight teeth. She addressed Marie like she was speaking to a small child, "Hello, dear, who are you? How may I help you?"

Marie cleared her throat. Suddenly she was transported back to her childhood, feeling like a child in a room full of adults expected to recite a poem or sing a show tune. "Mrs. Milton, my name is Marie Clyde. I attended high school with Rose. I wanted to tell you how sorry I am about her death. She was very sweet." For a moment, Mrs. Milton's perfect façade slipped a bit and tears appeared at the corner of her eyes. Then she quickly wiped the edge of her eyes with her perfectly manicured index fingers. She tilted her head to the right and smiled at Marie, but her smile didn't reach the woman's eyes. "Thank you for that, my dear. Did you know my Rose well?" Mrs. Milton took a step closer to Marie, taking Marie's palm in her hand.

"I only knew her in high school. She and I ran in different groups, but she was always kind to me," Marie said to the woman. Mrs. Milton squeezed Marie's palm. Marie thought about what she remembered of Rose. The girl was gorgeous, but she'd never realized it. She had run around with a bunch of wild girls in high school, driving too fast, sneaking alcohol and kissing dangerous boys.

"She was my sweet girl. She trusted people; she thought everyone told the truth. How I wish she'd never got involved with those terrible boys in London. Just criminals, common street ruffians, pretending to be something... That was when she started using drugs." Mrs. Milton spoke as if she'd told this story a thousand times. Her gaze drifted from Marie, as she remembered the events. Her grip on Marie's hand tightened. "The last few years she was totally clean, but the damage was done to her liver. That slow poison got her and I lost my little girl..." Mrs. Milton rubbed the pin on her lapel and squeezed Marie's hand tightly with surprising strength.

Marie winced silently. Hank reached over and touched Mrs. Milton's shoulder. Mrs. Milton blinked and released Marie's hand with a warm smile.

"Thank you again for your condolences." Mrs. Milton pivoted on her heels and continued through the front doors of the museum with Hank following closely behind her. Lauren stood next to Marie and the two women watched the older woman leave.

"That's so sad for her. It was sweet of you to speak to her," Lauren mused. She patted Marie on the shoulder. Marie rubbed her hand, surprised it still hurt from the grip.

"It's really sad. She looks so together, but underneath she's hurting" Marie agreed solemnly with her sister.

"So, what should we see next?" Lauren asked as they walked away arm and arm. Marie felt instantly more cheerful with her sister there.

The two chatted animatedly while heading to the Central American pre-Columbian art section. Here they silently admired the artwork, stopping to read the descriptions. They moved quickly through the other exhibits and then exited the museum, heading out through the sculpture garden.

In the Sculpture Garden, under the massive live oaks, Marie and Lauren smelled a heavenly scent——beignets. The two followed the scent like bloodhounds, arriving at the old Casino in City Park. Here they found an iron table and ordered. The white-clad waiter arrived with the delicious donuts and laid them on the table with a flourish.

"I've been waiting all morning for these." Lauren closed her eyes as she bit into the steaming fried dough covered in powdered sugar. She smiled and a puff of powdered sugar escaped her beignet and covered her chin.

"Oh, Lauren." Marie laughed and dipped her napkin in her glass of water and handed the wet paper napkin to her sister. Lauren thanked her sister and wiped away the sugar. Marie sipped her coffee. Her eye caught the peristyle across the park from where they sat. A young woman in magenta yoga pants stood in the middle of the stone bandstand doing a yoga tree pose, her eyes shut. Lauren followed her sister's gaze.

"You know, you should do something like that," Lauren suggested. She bit down on her donut, and powdered sugar covered her lips like white lipstick. She wiped it away.

Marie scrunched her face in confusion, looking at the fit woman and then back at her sister, "No way. I couldn't do that. Everyone is watching and it's exercise."

Lauren rolled her brown eyes at Marie. "How do you know that you couldn't do it? You should try it. It might be fun." Lauren looked at the woman who was now in a downward dog pose. Lauren leaned her head to one side, "Looks like it would help with flexibility."

"I don't want to do that." Marie added another teaspoon of sugar to her coffee. Marie watched the woman contort her body into something that resembled a pretzel——a magenta pretzel.

"Well, what do you want to do?" Lauren asked, grabbing a second beignet from the plate. Marie was caught off guard by her sister's question. She put down her mug. She thought back to their conversation the night before.

"I'm not sure," Marie answered honestly. Lauren lowered the beignet from her mouth and sat up. "But I know I don't want to do that. Come on, Lauren; it's exercise in tight pants," Marie added, hoping the humor would distract her sister from the subject.

"Marie, why don't you try something new? Try something that you're interested in. You read and go to the museum in your free time. All we need to do is add a cat and you'll become a hermit." Lauren waved her hand around her head, causing powdered sugar to envelop her hair. "Think about it, what are you actually interested in? And don't say reading or visiting the museum."

Marie thought for a moment. "But I read really interesting books," Marie protested. Lauren flicked powdered sugar at her younger sister, resulting in scattered white specks on Marie's brown sweater. "Okay, okay; you know, I like travel. I told you that last night but…" Lauren picked up more powdered sugar, threatening her sister, "I'm scared."

"What are you scared of, Marie?" Lauren asked softly. Marie thought about the question and drew in a sharp breath. She wanted to respond with a silly retort.

"What if I try something and something bad happens? What if I'm just a boring failure? What you see really is what you get?" Marie said the last words with a mirthless laugh. "I try stuff… sometimes…" Marie added lamely.

Lauren dropped the sugar on the plate and wiped her hands. She cocked her head to the side, gazing at her sister. A crooked smile crept across her face as an idea formed. She bit into her beignet. Marie squinted at her sister, trying to decipher Lauren's expression.

"What?" Marie pressed her sister, but Lauren took another bite of the beignet.

"I just had an idea." Lauren reached for the last beignet, but Marie swatted her sister's hand from the plate. A puff of powder sugar rose from the small plate as Marie grabbed the last beignet.

Chapter 5

When Marie returned home, she flopped onto her couch and turned on her television. After five minutes of channel hopping, Marie turned off the television. She sat on the couch, wrapped in silence. She picked up her book next to the couch and read a paragraph or two, but she put the book down. What should she do now?

She pulled her phone from her purse and kicked off her shoes. She surfed the web for fifteen minutes, skimming articles on news sites and watching a cooking video on YouTube. She tossed the phone down next to her on the couch and crossed her arms. She was bored.

Sunlight streamed through the curtains. Marie stood up and crossed the room. She leaned against the windowsill, staring at a vibrantly colored crepe myrtle tree outside. The color reminded her of a Wet 'n' Wild lipstick color she'd once purchased when she was 14. She remembered the name: Pink Escapade.

She'd never worn it. Her mother wouldn't allow it. "Too

garish," her mother had said. Marie had ended up giving the lipstick to Lauren. Lauren gratefully snatched the lipstick from her little sister, slathered it on, and later kissed some boy.

A jogger ran along the sidewalk under the tree. The runner moved gracefully like a gazelle. Marie turned and looked back at her shoes. Maybe she should try to go for a run? She could get out, see the neighborhood, do something.

Marie returned to the couch. Maybe she was boring. The thought deflated her. She got up to put away her purse and shoes and saw the crumpled program from the museum. She remembered the kiss. She touched her lips. Maybe she wasn't *that* boring. A knock interrupted her thoughts.

Peeking through the peephole, she saw a police officer and the tall man in the suit from earlier in the day. She opened the door slowly and peered out. What did they want? Weren't they supposed to call first?

"May I help you?" Marie asked, uncertain she really wanted their answer.

The man in the suit cleared his throat. "Ms. Clyde, we need to speak to you. May we come inside?" His grey eyes pierced her like daggers. This guy was intense.

"Please come in," Marie invited them with a wave into her small apartment and led them to the couch. Neither man sat, so Marie stood as well.

"What's going on?" Marie asked. Marie looked down at her bare feet. The tall man's gaze followed her own.

"My name is Donald Harris. This is Officer Davis. We met earlier today. May we look around your apartment?" She nodded and then Marie thought briefly about the state of her bedroom. Had she picked up her pajamas from this morning? Then it occurred to her that they weren't looking at her pajamas.

"Okay, what's this about? Why are you here? I thought you

would call or something—not just show up." Marie crossed her arms across her chest to try to appear calmer than she felt. Officer Davis immediately walked into her bedroom and started looking for something. She resisted the urge to follow him. Harris walked immediately to her low bookshelves, touching the binding of each book.

"Ms. Clyde, as you know, from your visit to the Museum earlier today, an item was stolen from the small Fabergé collection at the New Orleans Museum of Art. I found it curious that you were at the museum both yesterday and earlier today. After reviewing the security footage, it seems you had some sort of episode or 'accident' at the museum yesterday?" He looked at her with suspicion. He pulled the same small notebook from his coat pocket and poised his pen to write.

"Yes, I was there yesterday. I went on my lunch hour. I like to go to that room." He immediately began to write furiously. Marie leaned forward, trying to figure out what he might have written. He pulled his notebook back. He scowled at the page and wrote more.

"So, you visited the Fabergé room? And you also visited the control room, 'recovering' from a fall?" The tall man wiggled his fingers on either side of his head to denote quotation marks when he said "recovering." He tapped his pen on the pad. He took a step towards her and leaned down, stretching his neck. He reminded her of a menacing ostrich.

"Uh, yes, I also visited the control room. I fell down the last stair in the main lobby and hit my head. They took me to the control room to recover," she answered quietly. Unconsciously, she touched the slight red bump on her forehead. His grey eyes searched her face. She could feel her cheeks turning red. He leaned a little closer, as if inspecting the red bump on her forehead.

"So, you admit to being at the museum, in the Fabergé room and the control room?" He again tapped his pen on the pad. He raised an eyebrow at her. She opened her mouth to respond, but the other officer entered the room and shook his head. Mr. Harris slumped his shoulders in disappointment, looking to Officer Davis he pouted, "You didn't find anything?"

Finally, what was happening started to register with Marie. This man thought that she was involved with the theft at the museum. This was preposterous. "Do you think that I had something to do with this theft? That's ridiculous. I returned to work afterwards. There are a dozen people in my office."

"What did you do after work, Ms. Clyde?" Mr. Harris leaned in, awaiting his "ah-ha" moment.

"My sister came over and we drank for a couple of hours," Marie answered. Mr. Harris sucked in a breath. "We ordered Chinese for dinner. I think that I have a receipt in the kitchen…" Marie pointed to the kitchen counter.

At her answer, Mr. Harris looked even more sullen. He closed his little notebook and put it back in his pocket. Officer Davis looked at Marie and shrugged. Marie had to resist the urge to roll her eyes at his petulant child look. She would have just showed them both the door, but now her curiosity was piqued about the crime.

"You have a lot of questions for me, Mr. Harris, but I have a question for you. Who are you and what do you have to do with this? I can tell Officer Davis is a police officer, but what do you do?" Marie leaned toward the tall man. Harris pulled the cuffs of his blazer while he thought a moment about Marie's questions.

"To answer your questions, Ms. Clyde, I am an art theft detective. I've been hired by the museum and the family that loaned the item to aid in the recovery and restoration of the

Milton Red Fabergé Box back to the New Orleans Museum of Art." Marie's eyes widened.

"They stole my Fabergé box?!" Marie exclaimed in distress before she could stop herself. The two men exchanged a glance. "I mean, that's terrible. I really like looking—only looking—at that Fabergé box, in particular, not stealing it." She shook her head and could hear Officer Davis snort a laugh. The men looked like they might get up, but Marie wanted to know more.

"Would you two like some coffee?" Marie offered. The two men brighten up, while she began her coffee maker and pulled out some mugs. She gestured for the two men to be seated. Harris examined the spines of the four books stacked on the table next to her couch.

As she walked over with two mugs, she asked: "How did you get involved in that line of work? How long have you been doing it? Are you good at it?" She handed the men their mugs. Harris gingerly placed a book back in place. Marie wondered which one he'd held. Marie sat in her overstuffed chair, tucking her feet under the chair.

Harris sighed, but she could see a twinkle of amusement in the man's grey eyes, "I actually worked for the FBI for many years, in particular in cases having to do with counterfeits and fraud, but I also have an art history minor. I work for insurance companies and museums mostly and I'm very good at what I do, and I've been doing it ten years now. Do you have any more questions for me?" He blew on the coffee and took a sip. A grin replaced the grimace on his face for just a moment.

Marie observed the man for a moment. When his face relaxed, his face was pleasant, framed by salt and pepper hair and rectangular-framed glasses. He was obviously fit, but not from hanging out at a gym. Harris caught her staring and raised an eyebrow at Marie. She immediately repositioned herself in her chair, trying to cover what she was doing, but she knew that he knew she was looking at him.

"Do you suspect that I have something to do with this theft?" Marie asked earnestly. Marie wondered when anyone would have ever thought or suspected that she would be involved in a crime.

At this point, the silent police officer answered: "No, not really, we wanted to find out more about your time in the Faberge room." Mr. Harris glared at the officer.

"Oh, come on, Harris," said the officer, "You've seen this woman's financial and criminal record and her apartment. Do you still think she's involved in something like this?"

"You checked my criminal and financial records? Really? Did you find anything interesting?" Marie blanched. Officer Davis pulled on his collar when he realized what he'd said. Harris sat still as a statue with only his eyes moving to glare at Officer Davis.

Marie looked to Mr. Harris. Again, he didn't answer immediately; he tapped his fingers on the side of the mug. Silently he held the mug to his lips, slowly taking a sip. He shook his head. He put the mug on the table before him and again pulled out his small notebook. "Would you please tell us more about your time at the museum yesterday?" He settled himself on one of her overstuffed chairs.

"Uh, well, I went to the museum during my lunch hour. I go often, like I said before." Marie looked between the two men. Officer Davis nodded his head encouragingly. "I went to the Faberge room. I like to go there. I was looking at the exhibit and there was a man there." The two men leaned forward.

"What man?" Mr. Harris stopped writing in his notebook. "What did he look like? Give me a description."

"He was handsome, brown hair, great shape, British accent.

He said his name was Paul. Why are you two acting so strange?" Mr. Harris scrutinized Marie's face. What was he looking at? Marie reached up and touched her nose.

"Because, you were the only person we could see on the security footage from yesterday anywhere near that room, Ms. Clyde." Mr. Harris answered. Whatever he was staring at on her face lost his interest and he again wrote furiously in his notebook.

"But, he was with me when I was in the control room," Marie insisted. The two men looked at each other in amazement. Harris stood up and walked to the apartment door; he pulled out his phone and stepped outside. Marie watched the man exit. What was he doing now?

"Do you remember what happened in the control room? Did the man touch anything? Could you have touched any of the computers?" Marie shook her head. Her shoulders slumped.

"No, I only remember waking up and he was with me. He was really nice." Red crept into Marie's cheeks as she thought about the kiss. The kiss had been amazing. *Had he just kissed her to distract her?* The thought was like a dagger to her heart.

Harris returned to the room. "It looks like someone in maintenance did see this mystery man and confirmed that he accompanied Ms. Clyde to the control room. There were quite a few folks gathered around where you fell. The crowd followed for a little bit until they got you to the door to maintenance. He assumed you and this mystery man were a couple and didn't think to mention it earlier." Mr. Harris rolled his eyes.

He looked around the apartment and raised an eyebrow. "Clearly you're not involved in this theft, Ms. Clyde. Just a few minutes here with you confirms for me that you're just an average bystander." Somehow, the way he said the words stung worse than if he'd suspected her of stealing a work of art. She was just an average bystander. Red rose again to her cheeks. "I'm sorry we wasted your time, Ms. Clyde. Thank you for your coffee."

Officer Davis stood up and placed his mug on the table. "We're sorry to have disturbed you." The two men turned toward the door.

"Wait! Maybe I can help you. Maybe I can help you figure out who that man was and where he was going. He must have been involved in the theft." Marie walked toward the men. *What was she doing? Why was she volunteering to help them? Harris was a rude grump who'd thoroughly dismissed her.*

Harris turned toward her and crossed his arms across his chest, "What could you possibly tell me about this man that would help me find him?" Marie leaned back and looked Harris in the eyes. God, he was intense.

"He uses Peaceful Lavender Mint shampoo. They sell that at the Ritz Carlton Spa." Marie placed her hands on her hips and leaned toward the glowering man.

Harris and Davis looked at each other and then Harris bellowed with laughter.

"Ms. Clyde, perhaps I spoke too soon," he said. "You are definitely not average. You must either have a good sense of humor or you're a regular Jessica Fletcher. Have a good day." He dismissed her and pivoted on his heel. Officer Davis shrugged his shoulders and handed her his business card. The two men left.

Marie's mouth gaped open. He thought she was funny? Or had that man just called her Jessica Fletcher? Was she Jessica Fletcher? Should she have been insulted? Mrs. Fletcher solved mysteries and wrote books. That was a pretty exciting life.

She sat back down on her couch and lifted the book that Harris had examined earlier. It was the Mrs. Pollifax mystery she'd finished last night. For a brief moment, she was a suspect in the theft of a Fabergé box and she had a dashing boyfriend—not a woman who spent most evenings reading about adventures. But reality soon returned and she looked around her apartment, filled with books and knickknacks. It was comfortable, but was it enough? She couldn't get that kiss out of her head. Her mind ran through different scenarios.

Perhaps she could just go by the hotel and see if he was there. Ask him about that kiss? Maybe she could find the Fabergé box and return it? She shook the thoughts from her head. She was being ridiculous. She would put all this foolishness out of her mind and focus on something else. Her fingers tapped on the arm of the couch. Maybe a short drive to the Ritz Carlton and a few questions couldn't hurt?

Chapter 6

The lobby of the Ritz Carlton, New Orleans, exuded luxury and elegance. An arrangement of long stem white roses topped an ornate table in the middle. A smartly dressed concierge stood behind the gleaming oak front desk. Marie cursed her noisy shoes as she tapped across the marble floor. Usually she wore rubber-soled flats, but she'd decided to dress up to enter the fancy hotel. She stood at the front desk, waiting for the uniformed woman behind it to look up from her monitor. Marie tugged on the bottom of her blouse in the back and rubbed invisible wrinkles out of her black skirt. She cleared her throat.

At last, the woman looked up and gave Marie a tight smile. Marie smiled right back at her. Was she really going to do this? The woman raised her eyebrows, "May I help you?"

Marie cleared her throat again. She was unsure what she was doing. "I'm trying to find a man who's staying here at the Ritz Carlton." Marie mentally kicked herself. The concierge pursed her lips.

"I'm sorry, Madame, I'm not allowed to give out guest's

information." Marie nodded her head in agreement. Of course, the woman wouldn't tell her anything. Marie began to turn around and leave, but as she shifted her purse on her shoulder a plan began to form.

"I totally understand. Let me just look in my purse for his name. You see my boss asked me to deliver this gentleman some papers that we were preparing for him. I was supposed to take them to him earlier, but I didn't, and I think he's leaving town. What is his name? Paul something? Where is that paper? I think he's British, really good looking, blue eyes, looks like Javier Bardem?" Marie began rummaging through her purse for the imaginary papers. Marie could see the conflicted look on the woman's face. She needed to lay it on thicker: "I need to get these to him or I just know my boss will fire me. Why didn't I write this on my hand?" She let out a little sniff.

"Ma'am, I can tell you that we do not—nor did not—have any Englishman named Paul Something staying with us at this time. Are you sure you have the right first name? It kind of sounds like you're describing Mr. Mountbatten..." The woman immediately slapped her hand across her mouth, her eyes getting large.

Marie looked at the woman. The name was unusual and familiar. She'd heard it before. Could this be the same person as Paul? Like a lightning bolt, she remembered where she'd heard the name before: "Is his first name Philip? Philip Mountbatten?" The concierge's eyes widened, confirming Marie's suspicion.

Marie smiled at the name. She remembered hearing the family name of Prince Philip while watching a documentary on PBS. "Is Mr. Mountbatten still staying at the Ritz? I do hope I caught him before he left..."

"I'm sorry. He left this afternoon for the airport." The

concierge shrugged sympathetically. Marie nodded sadly. That was it. Nothing more to do. "He did ask me to send on a couple of packages for him. I just sent those on their way, but perhaps I could send on your papers as well?" The concierge added help- fully.

Marie tried to control her enthusiasm. "That would be fabulous, but I'd need to be sure that it gets to him. Which address is that?" The concierge immediately crossed her arms. "I mean, are his packages headed to the same address as his office in—gosh—was it the Geneva? Or maybe Rome? Geez…" Marie let her voice drop as again she began to rustle through her purse.

"In Paris?" The woman offered as if on cue.

"Of course, the Paris office, on Rue de Rivoli?" Marie tossed out the only street name in Paris that she could remember from reading that she could think of to keep the chatty concierge going. The woman looked down at her monitor and tapped on the keyboard.

"No, that doesn't sound right. It's Rue Marguerite. Here it is—Numero 3, Rue Marguerite! Do you want to give me those papers?" Marie memorized the address as she thought of a hasty fib.

"You know what, I'd better check with my boss first. That's such a good idea, but I better go, thank you." Marie pivoted on her heel and bolted from the lobby. She stood panting right outside the doors of the hotel on Canal Street. A red streetcar rattled past. This was crazy. Had she actually gotten the address for the mysterious Paul in Paris?

Marie turned over the information in her head as she wandered down Canal Street toward the parking lot. What was she doing trying to find this man who'd kissed her? Was she that desperate? Could he really have been involved in the stealing of the Fabergé Box from the museum? If Paul was his real name, why was he using a fake name at a hotel? Why did she care?

Marie shook her head, trying to clear her thoughts. Why was she thinking about this? This situation didn't involve her. She opened the door to her car and sat down. She pulled the visor down and checked her face. Was this the face of a woman who pursued strange men?

Chapter 7

Paul settled into his airline seat, snapping his seatbelt. He flipped open a magazine, only half reading an article about some vapid pop star. He tried to exude calm, but inside he replayed the last twenty-four hours in his mind. Usually the retrieval—as he referred to it—went smoothly.

He'd returned to the museum late in the evening and entered the building with ease, perhaps too much ease, he thought in hindsight. He'd uploaded a virus that shut down the alarm and camera system while the cute brunette was passed out in the control room. As he made his way through the museum in the dark, he'd entered the Impressionists room for his items.

He'd lifted the small Cassatt off the wall, carefully popping it from the frame. He'd laid it gently against the wall while he'd replaced a copy in its frame and re-hung the painting. He repeated this process twice more in the room.

Carrying the three small paintings, he'd padded softly along the wall to his final stop. He'd frozen when he'd heard the sound of breaking glass. Tiptoeing to the doorway, he'd peered in the room and was amazed at what he saw.

"Idiot! Grab the box and let's go!" A large black-clad figure roughly shook a smaller man who'd looked down incredulously at glass covering his dark shoes.

"Sorry, boss. I got it." The little man snatched the box off its perch and shoved it into a velvet bag.

"Be careful," hissed the larger man, "we need to get out of here before he arrives. I know Paul's going after it too." Paul leaned back against the wall, listening to the two men jostling in the room. He recognized the voice. Paul gritted his teeth in disgust and quickly ran for the stairs and toward the front doors.

Slipping out the building, he made his way to his car parked across from the Botanical Gardens in City Park. Pulling out his phone, he dialed 9-1-1, reported the theft and threw the phone out the car window as he drove over the bridge of the lagoon, waiting just long enough to hear it plop into the water below.

Paul leaned back in the leather seat. He was supposed to pick up the box. What was LaCroix doing there? Had the buyer hired him as well? After all these years, the two had never crossed paths, and Paul didn't want to cross paths with the man now.

LaCroix was nothing but a low life criminal and lousy thief to boot who looked like a young Marlon Brando but with crooked teeth. Thinking about LaCroix or Scott Cross (as he was called when the two were in their twenties) made Paul grind his teeth. LaCroix was pushy and brash, always getting in fights, always pulling one scheme or another. Paul would know, because the two of them used to run together with a gang in London. They'd grown up two doors apart on Kings' Court Lane.

Paul remembered his father warning him to leave Cross alone. "That boy's trouble; stay away from him," his father would shake his head and mutter, constantly tinkering or cleaning his tools on the kitchen table. Every time his father would offer his warning, he would punctuate the point by adding, "Listen to me, Paul Philip Smith!" Paul would swat away his father's wise advice, grimacing at what he thought was a pedestrian name. At that point, Paul himself was becoming that teenager that parents warned their children about.

The last time he'd seen LaCroix was when LaCroix had started calling himself LaCroix. "It's more sophisticated because it's French for Cross. The boss says if I want to start making good money, I need to be classy to meet clientele." Paul remembered rolling his eyes at LaCroix, but in the pit of his stomach, he felt some dread. What had he meant about "clientele"? Paul didn't understand at the time, but he began to realize what it meant later. LaCroix's new gang weren't just picking pockets and breaking into cars for money.

LaCroix and Paul had done a small job together—breaking into a jewelry store two neighborhoods over. LaCroix told Paul the new boss had summoned Paul for a meeting. The boss was always having tea at some posh teahouse across from Harrod's.

When they'd arrived, someone had patted Paul down. Paul tried not to squirm in his suit, as the man sitting in the booth silently looked both Paul and LaCroix up and down. The squat man in a shiny silver suit whispered something Russian to one of the other men in a less shiny blue suit. Paul gulped.

The man in the blue suit stood up, struck LaCroix, and spoke: "You don't bring anyone to the boss like this and where is the jewelry?" He shook LaCroix and swung at Paul. Paul ducked just in time to miss the man's meaty fist.

"I got it! I got it! This is my friend Paul. He helped me with the job. I thought you should meet him," LaCroix offered, pulling his leather sack open and pulling out little black velvet bags and boxes. Another man hopped up and slapped LaCroix. Paul stepped back again, lifting his hands to protect himself.

"Where's the rest of it?" the boss said in a low growl. LaCroix hemmed and hawed and promised to bring the rest next week. The boss dismissed the two and Paul sighed with relief to leave the place. At that moment, Paul knew he needed to put some distance between himself and LaCroix or he was going to find himself on the wrong end of a beating or worse.

A week later, Paul had successfully dodged his friend, but decided he needed to come clean. He needed to tell LaCroix that he didn't want anything to do with those gangsters. Paul entered the seedy club in Croydon where LaCroix wanted to meet. However, what he found was LaCroix kissing Paul's new girlfriend. The willowy, shy brunette threw her arm over LaCroix's shoulders and swayed. When she leaned back from LaCroix, Paul could see the ruby brooch that he'd bought her at a little jewelry store down the lane from his house. She'd giggled while he'd pinned it on her blouse, promising to always wear it and even calling her mother later that day to tell her about picking it out at the "quaint English store on Kings' Court Lane" while Paul had listened from her cramped dorm bed.

Paul stormed over to the two, demanding to know what was going on. The girl tried to stand up, but stumbled from off her stool. Paul looked into her glassy eyes and she just smiled at him. "He's French, I think. Or maybe he speaks French, just like my grandma could. She lived on Esplanade…" The girl stumbled away to the restroom, mumbling as she left.

"Cross, what are you doing? That's my girl!" Paul grabbed LaCroix's lapels and shook him. LaCroix just laughed, picked up his shot glass and slugged it down.

"She *was* your girl, mate. A University girl like that, she wants someone more sophisticated who can party, like me.

What are you, just some son of a locksmith?" LaCroix signaled the bartender for another shot. The man placed it down and LaCroix again chugged the shot, wiping the back of his hand across his mouth. Paul shoved LaCroix back on his stool. LaCroix slipped off his jacket and sauntered toward the restrooms. Paul stood there fuming. He gripped LaCroix's stool, feeling something in his jacket.

He pulled out a small velvet bag, pouring its contents into his hand. It had to be thousands of dollars' worth of diamonds! Paul looked around, wondering if anyone had seen him, then he pocketed the baggie and hurried out of the bar. That very evening, he headed back to Kings' Court, packed his few belongings, and headed to the airport, determined to put as much distance as possible between himself and his old life.

Paul pushed the memories away. He needed to get the box, and he knew LaCroix had the box. Maybe Paul could retrieve it from the thug before the exchange?

He sighed to himself. At least the other items were on their way. He'd pick up those items when he arrived back home, and have them ready for their buyers. He would need to figure out where LaCroix was going next, but he had a hunch it would be at the original drop off point.

Chapter 8

After her escapade, Marie was once again home and perched on her couch trying to read her romance novel. She had read the same paragraph about grasping the hero's throbbing something or other. Marie put down the book. If that section could not keep her attention, then she needed to do something different. She picked up Officer Davis' card from her coffee table and began to dial the number into her phone.

The phone rang three times and Marie thought that the voicemail would pick up when she heard Officer Davis' startled voice. Did she wake him up? She looked at her wristwatch to confirm the time. It wasn't that late.

"Uh, hello, Officer Davis, this is Marie Clyde. We spoke earlier today." Marie spoke in a rush.

"Of course, Ms. Clyde, how may I help you?" the officer asked sweetly, as if he were addressing a little old lady with a cat in a tree. He seemed alert now.

"Well, I wanted to tell you that I went to the Ritz Carlton to look for that Paul guy. He isn't calling himself Paul. He used a fake name—Phillip Mountbatten—and is probably on his way to Paris now. He's probably going to Number 3, Rue Marguerite." Marie blurted her story out as quickly as she could.

"Wait, you did what?" Officer Davis was much more alert now. He also sounded a bit alarmed.

"I said that I went to the Ritz Carlton to find that guy who was at the museum—Paul. I found out that he was using a different name there and is probably on his way to Paris." Marie recapped her story, hopping from her seat and pacing the room.

"You went to that hotel to find some random guy and discovered that he's going to Paris?" Marie shook her head at his question. *How was he not understanding this?*

"Yes," she answered. She rolled her eyes.

"Why would you do something like that?" Officer Davis asked incredulously. Marie had the distinct impression that he thought she was insane.

Marie wondered the same thing. She couldn't tell him that what she really wanted to know was why Paul had kissed her. "I thought that he might be involved in the theft. I pursued a lead," Marie answered in a huff and then sat back down on her sofa. Her answer sounded solid enough, though a little bit like a detective character from a *Law and Order* episode.

"Ms. Clyde, you aren't a police officer or investigator. That sounds really dangerous. You can't go to some random hotel looking for some random guy. There are easier ways to meet men," Officer Davis explained. Marie flushed red. At this moment, she was grateful that no one could see her.

"But, he may be involved in this crime," Marie exclaimed. Officer Davis let out a huff.

"I don't care. What you did was dangerous, Ms. Clyde. Leave the police work to the professionals. We don't need your help. We're already following a lead." He practically growled over the line. She felt like a scolded child.

"Oh, okay. I'm sorry I said anything," Marie meekly replied, "Have a good evening." Marie clicked off her phone and burst into tears.

Of course, he was right. She had no reason to get involved. She must have sounded like some crazed busybody. Marie wiped the tears on the back of her hand.

This has been a dreadful few days, Marie thought. Suddenly she felt very tired. She shuffled into her bedroom and glanced in the mirror. She was still dressed up from her jaunt to the Ritz Carlton. Her hair was all frizzed around her head and she looked weary. Who was she kidding? No one would want to kiss her now.

The next morning, Marie stumbled from bed to the kitchen. She scrolled through her emails on her phone while she fumbled with her coffeepot. The first few emails were junk. The next was some follow-up email from Michael's attorney confirming the date of their divorce. Marie opened the email and the attachment, reading the judgment. She closed the email and then she saw the email from David, her boss.

She sank onto a stool next to the counter. She read and re-read the email. The office would be closed for a week and half for renovations. Because no work or "only essential work" could be completed, one half of the staff, including Marie, would be on furlough until the official re-opening of the office in three weeks. There might also be a "restructuring" upon the reopening. Marie knew what that meant.

Marie angrily tapped in her sister's number. "Lauren, you're not going to believe this!" Marie practically shouted into the phone. She stomped around her kitchen, angrily opening the cabinet to take out a mug and starting her coffee.

"Good morning to you too, Sis. How are you this morning?" Lauren responded with an audible yawn.

"Sorry, good morning to you. How are you? Also, I'm on furlough for three weeks. Can you believe this?" Marie screeched into the phone. She shakily poured the coffee into her mug. She pulled a paper towel from the ring and wiped the spill, tossing the towel in the trash can.

"I'm fine, thank you for asking. I'm sorry to hear that, but you know, this isn't bad news. You and I could go on a trip together," Lauren answered. Marie was quiet a moment. "Hold on a second."

Marie could hear Lauren shifting the telephone. She lifted the mug to her lips and sipped. Yikes! It was hot. She blew on the liquid, listening to her sister. "This is the perfect time to tell you that after our conversation at City Park I decided to take action on your behalf, Marie." Marie's ears perked up, and she put down her coffee cup. What was Lauren talking about? She thought back to their exchange over beignets. Oh no, had Lauren signed up her for a yoga class? Lauren continued: "I've found two tickets to Paris for this evening. They were very reasonable if one already has an airline credit, which I did!" Lauren exclaimed triumphantly. Marie was dumbfounded.

"Wait, what?" Marie asked. She stood up, straightening her spine.

"I've found us tickets to Paris. We can go tonight. Why not? I've been thinking about this since we started talking about you running off to Paris with that mystery man who scares you." Lauren was excited. Marie could hear it in her voice, but Marie couldn't just leave on a moment's notice. But then, what did she have to lose? Should she take the trip? Marie tried to remember the last time she'd actually taken a trip or vacation.

"Lauren, we can't do that. I was just talking when I said that about that guy, but I didn't mean…" Marie thought back to her wild visit to the Ritz Carlton the night before. She was curious about the man. She tried shaking the thought from her head "This is crazy and expensive and…" Marie was trying to think of another excuse, but they all sounded so boring. "They'll probably order a full body search going through security. That would be awful!" That didn't sound boring or like anything Marie would like to experience.

"Maybe it would be fun depending on how cute the security guard was. Marie, it'll be fine. I had the credits because Lance and I had to cancel our trip to Colorado. It will cover one of our tickets and the other ticket wasn't that expensive. Marie, you haven't splurged on anything in six months because of the divorce and I know that you have a little savings for something special. This could be the 'something special,'" Lauren explained. Marie thought about that account. She'd saved it since before she and Michael had split. It was so they could do something fun together, then it became the "oh no, my husband wants a divorce" fund. As it turned out, Michael wasn't interested in a trip with her or in fighting over a bank account. He just wanted to be with someone else.

"Where would we stay? You just bought us tickets and we have nowhere to stay. This is a disaster waiting to happen!" Marie threw up another obstacle. Surely this would slow Lauren down. "There are probably no hotels anywhere nice. We could end up in a hotel above a wig shop or next door to a wig shop where we can't put our feet on the carpet." Marie wondered if such a place actually existed, but surely it must and it would probably be their hotel.

"Where would you like to stay in Paris?" Lauren asked. Marie had no idea. She needed to convince Lauren this was a bad idea, too risky. She thought about her conversation with the woman at the Ritz Carlton and wondered about the address. Surely it was some seedy part of Paris. Lauren would never stay somewhere seedy and Lauren would agree that this idea was ridiculous.

"I want to be near Number 3, Rue Marguerite. I heard about it somewhere, supposed to be an interesting neighborhood." Marie tossed the address out and smirked. An image of the neighborhood emerged in Marie's imagination filled with rat-filled sagging old buildings and street hooligans wearing berets. This would end all this frivolous planning, she thought, and Marie could get back to her complaining.

"Ooh, that is a cute little hotel!" said Lauren, "There! Booked. You must have been looking." Lauren squealed with delight. Marie dropped her phone. She scrambled to pick it up.

"Wait, there's actually a hotel at that address?" Marie asked. She ran to her laptop, booted it up and waited. She tapped in the address and—sure enough—the website for a charming boutique hotel appeared on her screen, Hotel Maguerite. Perhaps the universe was sending her a sign?

"I thought that's why you suggested it. Yes, it's a small hotel called Hotel Marguerite. It is in the sixth arrondissement, which is a pretty good spot for sightseeing. You can pay for the room. Now pack your suitcase for six days; we're going to Paris tonight!" Before Marie could squeak out another word, Lauren hung up.

Lauren had bought them tickets to Paris! This was crazy. The mysterious Paul was *in* Paris. Marie sat on the stool in her kitchen when her coffeepot clicked. She poured herself a second cup and realized her hands were shaking. She was so nervous she was shaking all over. A text dinged on her phone. It was from Lauren: "Go pack!"

Chapter 9

Harris and Davis had spent the whole morning at police headquarters re-watching the security footage from the museum on the day of the theft. Harris pulled his chair closer to the monitor and stopped the tape every few frames, trying to get a closer look at the mystery man. He muffled a laugh when he watched Marie fall on the last step, and then he rewound the film. The most either of them could tell from the tape was that the man looked to be about six feet tall and well dressed.

"It kind of looks like she's running down those stairs, like she's trying to get away from someone, hmm," Harris mused. "Why would she be running from this man? Why did she describe someone she was running from as handsome?"

Officer Davis watched the footage. He couldn't see what Harris was talking about. He pressed his lips together, unsure if he was supposed to respond to Harris' statement.

Later, the two men listened to the newly released 911 call about the theft. A slightly British accented voice reported seeing lights and people inside the museum. "Perhaps there's a theft happening," the voice suggested before cutting off. Suddenly, Harris remembered what Marie had said. The man in the Fabergé room spoke with a British accent.

After fielding seven phone calls from a museum patron who'd called Harris, upset about the theft, Harris silenced his cellphone. Then the two policemen returned to the museum. Officer Davis tried not to follow Harris around the small Fabergé room at the museum. Harris would stop suddenly and then move again. Twice Davis found himself stepping on Harris' heels. He finally decided he should find one spot and wait for Harris. Davis leaned against one wall and watched Harris' eyes scan the corners of the room.

Davis wanted to shout at the other man. Harris was infuriating. Davis realized the reason the investigator was so good at what he did was because he was so obnoxiously detail oriented. The man would inspect the straw he put in his iced tea, for goodness sake. Harris could probably tell him the temperature and density of the ice cubes in the tea, but Davis was over it. Harris had spoken less than fifteen words to him all day, but he expected Davis to cart him everywhere.

"Davis, let's take a walk around." Davis nodded and walked in step with Harris. The two exited the room and moved down the corridor to the next exhibit. This small room appeared to hold small medals and miniature paintings. Harris squinted at one, marveling at the tiny portrait of a grey-haired man wearing glasses. Again Harris stopped and started, scanning the corners of the room, and then with a sigh, moved to the next exhibit.

In the Impressionist room, Harris wandered close to the walls to inspect each painting. He paused before a painting by Mary Cassatt. The image was of a mother, hair piled on her head in what now would have been called a messy bun, holding her child on her lap. Harris leaned his head to one side, inspecting the painting. He reached out his hand and touched the painting. He rubbed his two fingers together.

"You can't do that," Davis exclaimed, ready to slap Harris' hand away. Harris looked at Davis with disgust.

"I can when it's a fake." Harris touched the painting again, wiping his fingers across the image. He showed Davis his two fingers. Davis leaned in closer and looked at the picture. It was a poster with globs of paint on it.

Harris reached into his back pocket and pulled out a handkerchief and wiped his hands. "I may need to speak with that weird woman from yesterday again, get a better description of that man she was with. I've seen a similar theft at another small museum in Spain about six months ago." Harris tucked his handkerchief into his pocket and pulled out his small notebook and began scribbling quickly. "What was her name?"

Davis pursed his lips, "You mean Ms. Clyde."

"Ah, yes, like Bonnie and Clyde—with all those books and her messy brown hair and freckles…" Harris described Marie perfectly. Harris flipped through his small notebook, "Do you have her number? I didn't take it down…" He began to write more questions.

"I have it," said Davis. "She called me last night about that man. She actually went to the Ritz Carlton to find him and said that he was using some fake name. Sounded crazy." Davis rolled his eyes recounting the conversation.

Harris stopped writing and set his stare on Davis, "What was the name?"

"Marie Clyde. You know, she seems a little bit like you. Kind of obsessive…" Davis mussed while Harris shook his head.

"No, not the brilliant Ms. Clyde, what was the fake name that man was using?" Harris' eyes widened with expectation.

"How would Ms. Clyde have known this person was using a

fake name?" he asked Harris, prompting a sneer from the man. "Phillip Mountain-something?" Davis answered and snapped his fingers trying to remember.

"Phillip Mountbatten?" Harris crossed his arms and shook his head, looking to the ceiling. Davis followed his gaze until he realized there was nothing on the ceiling.

"Yes, that's what she said. What does that mean?" Davis stepped back. Harris grimaced and pulled his phone from his coat pocket and dialed. Harris pivoted on his heel and bolted through the door.

Harris practically took the marble steps two at a time, running toward the front desk at the museum. Davis chased behind the tall man. Stopping at the desk, Harris demanded something from the volunteer behind the desk and she handed him the register.

Davis was breathless, standing behind Harris, trying to peer over the man's shoulder. "What? What is it?" He couldn't see what Harris was doing. Harris flipped through the pages of the visitors' register, scanning each line.

"Mountbatten is Prince Phillip's surname. At the other museum, the only clue or strange thing we could find was on the visitor's register. It seemed like a joke. 'Felipe Bourbon-Anjou' had visited the museum that week." Harris continued scanning and turning the pages.

"So, who is that?" Harris stopped on a page and turned the book so that Davis could read the page. He tapped his finger on the elegant signature: Phillip Mountbatten.

"Felipe Bourbon-Anjou is the King of Spain. Phillip Mountbatten is Prince Philip, married to Queen Elizabeth. These are both charming museums, but I highly doubt that either monarch is visiting them. I think it's more than coincidence that they're both on the registers during the same week that the museums have thefts. We need to find out more about that man from Ms. Clyde."

Chapter 10

Marie folded her underwear and stuffed it into her suitcase. She looked down at her watch. She needed to leave her apartment in the next half hour if she was going to arrive at the airport on time. She hurried to her bathroom and tossed items into a zip-lock bag. She caught her expression in the mirror. She was grinning from ear to ear. She stopped for a moment to admire herself in the mirror when she heard the pounding on her door.

She peeked through the peephole. Officer Davis and Mr. Harris stood looming. Harris peered at a spot on the door and a huge gray eye spied through the peephole back at Marie. Marie's grin immediately became a frown. Marie opened the door, "May I help you, gentleman?"

Mr. Harris cleared his throat and smiled at Marie. Marie thought she could see every tooth in the man's mouth. He actually looked pained.

"Ms. Clyde, I was wondering if I might have a word with you. I would love to learn more about your experience at the museum on the day of the theft." His smile grew even toothier, if that were possible.

"There really isn't that much more to tell, Mr. Harris. I did go to the Ritz Carlton to try to see if I could run into him, but I told Officer Davis about that." Marie leaned on her doorway. She crossed her arms and realized that she was still holding a pair of socks in her hand. She returned to her bedroom and stuffed them in the suitcase.

"Would you tell me what you discovered at the Ritz Carlton?" Mr. Harris was practically fluttering his eyelashes at Marie when she returned to the living room. She rolled her eyes at him.

"I thought you said that I was acting dangerously and that I should leave the investigating to the professionals." Marie pointedly spoke to Davis. She again crossed her arms and looked between the two men. Officer Davis avoided her eyes and Harris pursed his lips. Marie shook her head: "I found out that the man I met, was calling himself Phillip Mountbatten at the Ritz Carlton. He left town yesterday and I believe he's headed to Paris. He had the concierge send his packages to his "office" in Paris which turns out is a hotel there." Marie was practically breathless when she finished her story.

Harris was busy writing the information in his tiny notebook. "What's the name of the hotel in Paris? Or did they tell you the name of it? Maybe a neighborhood or address?" Harris asked.

"Hotel Marguerite on 3 Rue Marguerite," Marie answered. "Gentleman, if that's all, I really need to finish packing. I have a flight to catch." Marie motioned to close the door and Harris placed his hand on the door jam.

"They told you all that? The concierge told you the name of the hotel and its address?" Harris seemed to speak to himself, then squinted at Marie: "Where are you traveling to, Ms.

Clyde?" Harris asked Marie. He leaned forward. Marie leaned back.

"Funny you should ask. My sister and I are going to Paris. Have a great day." Again, Marie attempted to shut the door.

"Ms. Clyde, did you just say you're going on vacation to Paris?" Harris pushed past her into the apartment. Marie looked down at her watch.

"Yes, my sister came up with the idea and she had some flight credits, so…" Marie stopped talking. Harris' eyes felt like laser beams on her.

"Ms. Clyde, are you attempting to investigate the theft at the museum? You went to that hotel yesterday." Harris again loomed over her. Marie swallowed hard and looked again at her watch. She still had time.

"I admit that I am curious, but it's just a coincidence. My sister thought a last minute trip together would be fun, and I agree." Marie sounded cheerful. She smiled at both men. Harris frowned and turned away, pacing her small living room.

Harris looked at her, "Where will you be staying in Paris?" Again, Marie gulped.

"Hotel Marguerite. It has three stars," she chirped, hoping that Harris didn't remember the address and name she'd just given him.

"Let me guess, it's just a coincidence that you chose to stay at the same hotel in Paris where you believe your mystery man is headed?" Harris crossed his arms and released a sigh. Marie smiled and shrugged. "Miss Clyde, you are playing a dangerous game, pretending to be a detective."

"Mr. Harris, I'm not pretending to be anything. I am going on a trip with my sister. Now, if you don't have any other questions for me, I need to finish packing. If you need me, you know where I'll be staying and I'll return in a week." Marie walked to her door and opened it for the two men to exit.

"Why are you going there? Why are you following that man? Did something happen between you two?" Harris demanded, wagging a finger at Marie. Both Davis and Marie leaned back from him. Red crept into Marie's cheeks. "So, something did happen?" Harris pressed his palms together and stepped closer to Marie.

"That's really none of your business. I need to leave." Marie motioned toward the open door, but Harris stood straight up, looking down his nose at Marie.

"You like this guy. He said or did something to intrigue you, and I'm going to figure it out." Harris almost spat the words. Marie flinched, trying to avoid imagined or actual spittle.

Harris stormed out with Davis scurrying behind him. Before Marie could close the door, Harris swung around and looked at Marie: "I will be keeping an eye on you, Ms. Clyde."

Harris sat stonily quiet, his arms crossed, as Davis pulled the car from the curb. He reached into his breast pocket and pulled out his notebook and began flipping through the pages. *What did he really know about this Marie Clyde woman?*

He re-read his notes and laughed mirthlessly. On the bottom of his third page of notes about the woman, he saw what he wrote: "Boring." Another word popped into his head: "Lonely." He immediately scribbled the word down and added: "like me" before he scratched the last two words. *Why had he written that?*

"Where are we headed, Mr. Harris?" Davis interrupted Harris' thoughts. Harris turned and studied the other man's profile. Davis appeared bored. Scratch that. Davis was definitely bored.

"Just drop me at my hotel. I need to make some travel

arrangements." The two continued to the Hampton Inn on St. Charles Avenue. Harris hardly waited for the car to stop before flinging open the door and running through the front doors of the hotel, heading for his room.

Back in his room, he loosened his tie and sat on the edge of his bed, wondering what he should do next. His thoughts drifted back to Marie Clyde. He scanned the beige room and contrasted it with the vibrant blue and stacks of books he saw in her apartment. This space was tidy and sparse, not unlike his empty apartment in Chicago. Marie Clyde's space was messier, but it felt warm.

The woman appeared of sound mind. She certainly was observant and smart. Ms. Clyde had managed to figure out that their thief had probably stayed at the Ritz Carlton based on his shampoo brand. She was attractive, so why would she seemingly chase after this thief? She could probably have any man she wanted. Why did that bother him? Maybe because she was so smart? Did she not realize that she was pretty and smart?

He shook his head. Where had that come from? He remembered that she had a coffee stain on her shirt, for crying out loud. *She was boring*, he told himself again. Still, objectively, she was somewhat cute. He reassured himself that that was all that he was thinking. Unless, of course, she was involved with this mystery man.

If she were involved with the man, maybe she could lead Harris right to the thief and right to the artwork? He wasn't the type of person to take a lot of risks. He was cautious and thorough. That's what made him good at what he did, but every now and then one needed to take a risk or follow a hunch. He pulled out his phone. Maybe he needed to take a risk on Ms. Clyde.

Chapter 11

Marie arrived at the airport in record time and parked her car in long-term parking. She made her way to the terminal and began to check in at the counter. She looked around the airport for her sister while answering the desk clerk's questions. She handed over her luggage and took her ticket from the clerk.

Again, she glanced down at her watch. It wasn't like Lauren to be late, especially late for a flight. Perhaps, Lauren was already at the gate? Marie headed toward the line at security.

She flipped through the pages of her passport. It had been years since she'd last used her passport for a trip. This passport was new. She remembered renewing it last year in anticipation of taking a trip with Michael.

She remembered returning from the post office after sending off her old passport. Michael was on his laptop in the dining room. She was so excited to plan a trip with him, but he just looked up at her and frowned. He didn't want to go where she wanted to go, besides he didn't even speak the language. When the little passport book arrived, Marie tucked it in its manila envelope in her underwear drawer.

Marie made her way closer to the security agent, her passport and ticket ready to present. Her hand was shaking. What was she thinking? She didn't speak French. This was a bad idea. She should just go home. She could read a book, maybe take a walk, head to the library book sale this weekend. Marie began to turn around when she saw Harris in the line. He was smirking at her!

"Next, please!" The security agent waved Marie to her. In a rush of decision, Marie handed the woman her documents and then headed to the x-ray machines, slipping off her shoes and tossing her purse and carry-on on the conveyor belt. She looked over her shoulder. There he was again, smiling like a shark at her.

"Excuse me, ma'am, would you please follow me over to the side? We would like to conduct a short search of your person and your luggage," the guard informed Marie. Marie nodded. Isn't this just what Marie had warned her sister would happen if they went on this trip?

A broad-shouldered woman with bright blue eye shadow and her hair in a high bun waved Marie out of the line. The woman patted her down. Her expression was completely blank. She then led Marie to her luggage on a table. The woman pawed silently through the luggage.

Out of the corner of Marie's eye, she saw Harris making his way through security. She noticed a smirk on his rugged face. Marie turned back to the table as the security officer pulled two Harlequin paperbacks from her carry-on, holding them up. The woman raised an eyebrow to Marie.

"They are research for my trip." Marie shrugged her shoulders. The woman smiled and returned the books to Marie's bag. She handed Marie her luggage and Marie swung around, right into Harris. She smiled as heat radiated from her cheeks. She looked down at her feet and scurried to a nearby bench and put on her shoes.

After her humiliation at security and having put on her shoes, Marie checked her ticket, looking for her gate. She moved quickly down the corridor to her gate and when she found it, she sat down next to the windows. She scanned the area. Harris had disappeared. She supposed he must be traveling somewhere else. Again she checked her watch. Where was Lauren? Her phone rang in her purse.

"Hello!" Marie answered relieved her sister had called. There was a loud cough and snort in the background coming from the other end of the line. "Lauren, is that you?"

"Marie, I have some good news and I have some bad news. Good news is Lance and Robert both came home today, right after we spoke this morning. The bad news is that they both have the flu. I can't leave them here alone. I'm so sorry I can't come with you to Paris." Marie could hear Lauren speaking softly to someone with her and then the individual coughing loudly. Lauren whispered into the phone: "There's vomit everywhere! I mean, did Lance eat a boot this morning? How can so much vomit come out of one person, let alone two?" Marie wrinkled her nose in disgust at the image.

"But, Lauren! I'll be there by myself. I don't speak French!" Marie almost shouted into her phone. She looked to her left and right. A grey-haired woman with a blue scarf stared at Marie. Marie smiled at the woman and lowered her voice, "What should I do? I told you that I was scared to do this by myself."

"Marie, you aren't heading to Mars. It's Paris. You always talk about traveling; now you're doing it. You'll be fine. Oh no, no, Robert! Aim for the toilet! Marie, I gotta go. Bye." The phone clicked off. Marie sat dumbfounded. Someone behind the counter announced the boarding of the plane.

Marie breathed in and out. She felt afraid. She was sweating. Marie's phone dinged with a text. It was from Lauren. "You can do this. You'll love it!" Marie smiled down at her phone, clicked it off and boarded the plane. She was doing this.

She moved slowly through the tight aisle to her seat. Reaching her row, she saw two passengers already in their seats; her seat was in the middle. Marie controlled a sigh. She wrestled her carry-on into the overhead compartment and squeezed over the man on the aisle seat. She wedged herself between the two.

After settling into her seat, Marie turned to the man in the aisle seat. He released a soft snore from under a sleep mask and a pair of noise cancelling headphones. Marie suspected that he couldn't possibly have fallen asleep that fast, considering the plane was still boarding. On her other side, a petite grey-haired woman stared out the window over the wing, watching the airline workers load the plane.

Marie pulled the airline magazine from the pocket in front of her knees and flipped through it. She could tell from a glance there was nothing in pages of interest to read. She looked up when the captain announced the doors of the airplane had closed. The flight attendants reminded passengers to buckle their seat belts and began their safety demonstration. Marie watched intently and then glanced down at her watch—only five minutes had passed. This was going to be a long connecting flight to Atlanta.

"Are you a nervous flyer? You seem like a nervous flyer." A small voice spoke into Marie's ear. Marie turned her head to the owner of the voice. The petit grey-haired woman leaned against the small window and examined Marie with piercing brown eyes. She wagged a finger at Marie, "Yes, indeed, I called it.

I could tell. Is this your first time on a plane, dear?"

Marie couldn't help but grin at the older woman. She shook her head, "No, I've flown before." Marie thought about the last trip she'd taken. She and Michael, her ex, had gone on their honeymoon to Cancun. As soon as that plane had taken off, Michael had started barfing in the lavatory and he didn't stop until after the third night of their trip. She should have taken that as a sign then and there. She frowned.

"So, you are a nervous flyer?" The woman offered, raising her thin eyebrows. "You seem unsure about something. You might as well tell me." Marie laughed. "I'm serious. This is a two-hour flight. You can either sit there in a bundle of knots, listening to old Rip Van Winkle or you can make the time fly lickety-split by talking to me." The woman snapped her fingers. Marie considered the offer.

"I guess I am a little nervous." Marie spoke slowly, adjusting in her seat to look at the woman.

"I knew it. I just knew it. You know, there's nothing to worry about. Flying is very safe, much safer than driving. Or maybe much safer than me driving all the way to Atlanta to see my grandchildren," The woman stopped for a beat waiting for Marie to laugh at the joke which Marie obliged with a small titter, "But seriously, it's much safer. All the flight attendants and pilots are well trained. I've taken this flight twice a year for the last eight years and there hasn't been one crash." The woman turned and looked out the small window. Outside the clouds stretched out in hues of blue and orange and red. "Wow, would you just look at that?"

Marie peeked over the woman's shoulder.

"Beautiful." She looked back at the magazine in front of her. Would she be able to retrieve her books from her carry-on? She began to reach for the magazine when the woman turned back and looked at Marie.

"Hmm…you still look nervous." The woman's piercing eyes focused on Marie's forehead. Marie reached up and touched her forehead, realizing she was wrinkling her brow. She tried to rub the crease out. "That won't work. Believe me, I've tried." Again the woman waited a beat and Marie laughed. "My name's Charlotte Green. What's your name?"

"My name's Marie Clyde. It's nice to meet you, Ms. Green." Marie shook the woman's hand. "So, you're headed to Atlanta to see your grandchildren?"

Ms. Green smiled broadly, clearly thinking about them. She nodded as she spoke, "Yes, I have three who live there with my daughter and son-in-law. I also have two who live here with my son and daughter-in-law. I try to see them as much as possible. I think that everyone should be so lucky to have grandchildren." Marie liked the woman's answer. "Are you traveling to Atlanta for work?"

"Oh no, it's the first leg of my trip. I'm flying to Paris." Marie realized that this was the first time that she'd said her destination aloud. "I'm going to Paris," Marie repeated it like a mantra.

Marie's seatmate leaned back in her seat and rubbed her hands together in delight, "Oh, Paris! What an extraordinary delight! Are you going for work or pleasure?" Ms. Green emphasized the word *pleasure*.

"I guess I'm going for fun. My sister and I were supposed to go together. She just sprang this on me today." Marie thought about the morning phone call and the hurried packing.

"You're going with your sister? Where is she?" Ms. Green stretched in her seat looking for Marie's sister.

"We were supposed to go together, but she backed out. So here I am," Marie answered. The other woman was quiet for a moment.

"She was afraid," Ms. Green stated with an absolute certainty. Marie opened her mouth to correct the woman but then she closed her mouth. "Fear is a terrible thing. It keeps you on the ground and not in Paris. Have you ever visited there before?"

"Just once, it was part of a tour in college. We only stayed two days and then headed to our next stop in Rome," Marie said. "I'm not sure our group ever got off the bus."

"You barely got to see anything in that time," said Ms. Green. "You poor dear, but now you'll make it right. You're off to Paris and you'll see everything. How I envy you!" Ms. Green shook her fists.

A flight attendant interrupted the two to take their drink order. "You know what? We need to have champagne for your trip! You are doing something wonderful and fun and exciting and we should celebrate. I insist!" She ordered two champagnes and pulled two coupons from her pocket. "I have almost eighty of these drink tickets socked away."

The flight attendant returned with two plastic cups of champagne and handed them to Marie and Ms. Green. The two clinked cups and sipped the bubbly drink. The man on the aisle seat lifted one corner of his eye mask and gave his two seatmates a dubious stare before covering his eyes.

"Ms. Green, it sounds like you've been to Paris quite a bit. Where would you suggest I go?" Marie sipped her drink.

Ms. Green held the cup between her hands and thought, "I have. I first went with my husband on our honeymoon and then six times after that. If you can believe it. I love Paris. That's one of the two things I have in common with Audrey Hepburn." Ms. Green sipped her champagne.

"What's the other thing you have in common with Audrey

Hepburn?" Marie asked curiously.

"My good looks, of course!" The two broke out in loud giggles. Rip Van Winkle glared from under his headphones. "Back to your question, what to see in Paris? Let me think, let me think. Of course, you must go to the Eiffel Tower, the Champs Elysées, the Louvre but you really must just stroll down those boulevards with your parasol, stopping for vin at each café and soak it all in."

"That's all on my list. Of course, you're right. I'm nervous, not about the flying, but about this trip." Marie spoke softly. Ms. Green listened intently to Marie. "It's strange doing this alone, kind of scary."

"Of course, it's scary. Terrible things could happen to a single woman traveling alone. You could get lost or robbed or kidnapped. Have you seen that film with Liam Neeson?" Ms. Green gulped down her champagne and waved to the flight attendant.

"You aren't very reassuring, Ms. Green." Marie wrinkled her brow. She hadn't considered getting kidnapped. That seemed like a distinct possibility considering the situation.

"It is scary, Marie, but it also may be wonderful and fun. You may get lost and find a treasure. You might get robbed and lose some inhibitions. You most certainly could be kidnapped and make a new friend. This is your trip and it's all up to you to make it work." Ms. Green gently patted Marie's arm on the armrest. She was silent for a moment. "You know, years ago, I went and I got lost for hours in Paris. Mind you, my French is not great, but folks were not helping either. I felt so frightened and unsure, and I remember leaning against this one building for a moment to gather myself. Some tourists stopped right in front of me and snapped a picture. I turned around and I couldn't figure out what they were taking a picture of so I asked and thankfully they spoke English. Turns out, what I was leaning against wasn't a building at all. It was just a façade that covered one of the ventilation shafts of the Metro." Ms. Green nodded her head. "You can look this place up; I think it was in the 10th arrondissement. You would never have guessed it was fake. That tourist worked for the Metro in his home country and that was how he knew about it. We ended up having a coffee together and they helped me find my hotel."

"That sounds pretty interesting." Marie mentally placed the strange little fake building on her list. She would try to find it. Still fears creeped into her mind, but Ms. Green again patted Marie's arm.

"You'll be fine. It will be an adventure!" Ms. Green reassured Marie. The two clinked plastic glasses again.

Chapter 12

Marie emerged from her international flight bleary-eyed, clutching her purse and carry-on tightly to her chest. Charles du Gaulle airport was bustling and drafty. She followed the crowd to Customs with her passport ready, inwardly kicking herself for not taking a French class in high school.

Marie sailed through Customs and grabbed her suitcase from the luggage carousel. She looked around for the shuttle company, when she read her last name written on a white board held by an eager driver in a black buttoned up shirt and skinny jeans. Maybe she was going to be okay. She waved to the driver and walked over. The young man immediately blurted out an incomprehensible line of French.

"I said, Hotel Marguerite, no?" The man repeated in English and smiled at her. Marie laughed and nodded her head. The two took off to his van. He attempted to engage her in small talk, but she felt so weary that she could only answer yes or no to his questions. He placed her suitcases in the back and invited her to sit down. Only one other person was in the van, seated next to the driver. Something was familiar about him.

"How was your flight, Ms. Clyde?" the voice in the front seat asked. Harris turned his head towards the backseat and smiled at Marie.

"What are you doing here?" Marie asked in complete shock. She felt self-conscious and cupped her palm over her mouth trying to smell her breath.

"I thought I'd just take a little trip to Paris to see if I could recover some stolen artwork. Isn't the better question: What are you doing here?" Before Marie could answer, the young driver hopped into the van and snapped on his seatbelt. Harris turned back around in his seat.

"As you say in the United States," the driver said, "away we go! How lucky that I only have one stop today. You both stay at the same hotel. Is it your honeymoon?" The driver pulled into traffic with a jolt. Marie gripped her seat to keep from sliding into the window. "Paris is the city of love…"

Neither Marie nor Harris could correct the driver as he drove so fast. Marie was gritting her teeth and Harris was holding onto the dashboard and the side door handle as the two were rocked back and forth. The young driver chattered incessantly, while weaving in and out of traffic at speeds that would put the *Fast and the Furious* franchise to shame.

Marie was breathless when the driver turned onto Rue Marguerite, screeching to a halt at the entrance of Hotel Marguerite. If one blinked, he or she might have missed the stenciled sign and simple glass doors of the hotel. Marie gathered her baggage and looked around the neighborhood. In one direction there was an adorable bread store, an impressive looking restaurant, and maybe a newspaper stand. In the other direction there appeared more residential structures with grey stone apartment buildings barely a sheet of paper apart.

Marie entered the double set of sliding glass doors to the hotel. A tiny reception desk tucked into a corner on the right side beckoned. A colorful abstract painting covered the whole wall behind the desk. While the lobby was small, the space didn't feel cramped. There were several café tables and chairs and sofas along the wall. She noticed that someone was clearing away what smelled like a delicious breakfast. Her stomach rumbled as she neared the hotel registration desk.

A chestnut-haired woman with a burgundy scarf tied around her neck looked expectantly at Marie. Marie could not help but smile broadly at the woman. She looked like she could have fallen out of a fashion magazine. Marie sighed when reaching up to check her bun and discovered half her hair sticking out one side.

"May I help you?" the woman asked. She barely had an accent.

Marie nodded and replied with a weak: "Oui! Si vous plait." The woman stifled a giggle. "I have a reservation, un reservation. Je m'appelle Marie Clyde."

The woman began to type on her computer, somehow maintaining excellent posture. Marie rolled her shoulders. She felt like she'd been tied in a knot and then thrown in a washing machine. Her stomach grumbled again.

"Well, here we are, Ms. Clyde. Together again. Perhaps we should have breakfast or something because surely you can't check in just yet." Harris appeared right at Marie's side. He smiled down at her, but somehow the grin didn't meet his eyes. Marie looked at him, her mouth hanging open, unsure of what to say.

"How can you look so fresh after that flight and that car ride?" Marie didn't expect the words to tumble out her mouth, but she was jetlagged and starving. Indeed, he looked freshly showered with a hint of aftershave in a blue blazer and a white oxford cloth shirt. Marie looked down at her rumpled blue sweater and faded black slacks. Harris immediately turned toward the woman at the registration desk, but Marie could detect red creeping into his cheeks. She really needed a coffee.

"I'm sorry, Madame. Your room will not be ready until this afternoon, but you may leave your luggage here while you wait." A wave of weariness rolled over Marie. She had made it this far, but now she had to kill hours and she didn't actually speak French. Her stomach grumbled again.

"Do you have a map?" Marie asked the desk clerk. The woman gave a slight smile and handed her a map. Marie immediately opened it, oriented herself and then turned to the sliding glass doors leading outside.

"Looks like I have to wait as well; where are you going to go?" Harris once again stood right next to Marie. She looked up at his smug expression. She pressed her lips together, gripped her purse's strap and walked through the sliding doors.

The doors shut behind her with a whoosh of air. Marie stood dumbfounded on the sidewalk. The air felt cool. Would she need a sweater? Would she get lost? Marie began walking, at first unsure if she was heading in the right direction until she saw the sign for Rue de Sèvres. She was going to see the Eiffel Tower and find a macaroon. She could do this.

Her pace was leisurely as she looked for the right streets and stared up at the buildings. People moved around her like water around a stone in a stream. She stopped at a corner, admiring rows and rows of flowers. She looked up and she could see the Tower in the distance. She was obviously going in the right direction.

"So, are we going to the Eiffel Tower?" Again, Harris stood next to her. He was like a fly. Was the man tiptoeing behind her? She wanted to swat him.

"Are you following me?" Marie asked. She was not going to let the annoyance interrupt the beauty of the moment. Marie stared at Harris. The Eiffel Tower appeared to be sticking out of the top of his head. A giggle bubbled up out of her throat into a hearty laugh.

Harris looked around and down at his clothing. "What's so funny?" Marie cleared her throat and covered her mouth with her hand.

"You looked like the Eiffel Tower was sprouting from your head." Marie blurted out in a giggle. Harris wrinkled his brows, but she could see the corners of his lips upturn. She repeated he question: "Are you following me?"

"Yes, I guess that I am following you, Ms. Clyde." Harris took off his eyeglasses and wiped the lenses with a handkerchief from his back pocket. His wrinkled brow smoothed as he put the glasses back on. "So, where are we going this lovely morning in Paris?"

"If you must know, I am indeed heading to the Eiffel Tower to see it up close and I'm on the hunt for a macaroon. I'm starving," Marie answered Harris. The two stood on the corner and looked at each other while pedestrians walked around them.

"The last time I was in Paris, there was a food stand or cart near the foot of the Eiffel Tower that sold macaroons. We could go find it. I also think if we go down this boulevard, we'll get there faster." Harris pointed down a café-lined street.

"That sounds like a good plan, but why are you following me?" Marie cocked her head to one side and looked up at him.

"I'm curious." Harris smiled at Marie. This time the smile actually reached his eyes. She accepted his answer as the two strolled down the boulevard toward the Eiffel Tower. They chatted along the way. Harris pointed out small details in the architecture. Marie soaked in the sights, sounds, and smells with relish.

They arrived at the Eiffel Tower and the two fell into a hushed silence. They made their way to one side of tower. The area was a shady park, somewhat empty of tourists and food stands. Marie walked over to the chain link fence that kept people from actually touching the base of the tower and she looked up.

"Wow, I'm here. I am actually here. And I made it by myself," Marie spoke aloud. Her eyes filled with awe. She gripped the fence.

"I'm here too," Harris interrupted Marie's thoughts. She turned to look at him.

"I suppose you are here too. But why are you here? Maybe you could write something down in your little notebook about the moment," Marie joked, but Harris didn't smile. She didn't mean the words to sound as harsh as they did when she said them aloud.

"I beg your pardon, Ms. Clyde." Marie immediately realized that her words had stung him, but she wasn't quite sure why. He seemed so serious and tightly wound.

"I'm sorry. I didn't mean to offend you, Mr. Harris." Marie patted his arm and rested her hand for a moment. He looked down at her hand on his arm and then at her face. She immediately snatched back her hand. She pivoted and observed the green space behind them. There was an iron bench and she sat on it. Curiosity seized Marie: "What do you write in your little notebook?"

Harris' gaze fell on Marie, considering her. His hard expression softened, "I like to take notes so I can remember details. In my line of work, details can be very important. If you pay attention to them, you can solve any mystery." Harris had answered honestly. He couldn't remember the last time someone had been interested in what he did or how he did what he did.

"Have you always carried a little notebook and taken notes?" Marie imagined Harris as a little boy in an oversized suit, chasing other children with his notebook.

"I started carrying one when I joined the FBI. My partner insisted on it. He said it helped organize his thoughts and it would help me organize my own. So, like I said, details are important in my line of work. My notebook helps me." Harris spoke and Marie suspected that the man might snuggle with his notebook at night. At the same time, she admired his intensity.

"What detail did you write about me in your little notebook?" Marie asked playfully. She placed her palms on her hips and attempted to give a coy expression, but she couldn't hold the pose without giggling. Harris' face went blank.

"I didn't write anything about you," he answered earnestly. He looked surprised by her question, even shocked. Both looked away from each other.

Marie felt foolish for her bold question and straightened up on the bench. "Oh, I see. You didn't write anything? That makes sense because there isn't anything to write." Internally, Marie was kicking herself. *Why had she attempted to flirt with this man? Wow, that had been a disaster.*

"Yes, I didn't write anything," he paused, "but I did draw stick figures," Harris offered dryly. He pulled out the notebook from his pocket and walked toward her while opening it, "Would you like to see them? I think they're a good likeness of you. I used crayons…" Marie covered her face while she laughed.

"You're not who I thought you were." Marie smiled offering the compliment, surprised at Harris' humor.

"Likewise, Ms. Clyde." Harris sat next to her and gently patted her with his notebook. "Why did you come to Paris? Are you following that man?"

"I could ask you the same thing. Are you following that man?" Marie asked Harris, turning the question to him. He pressed his lips together. She could see he was considering whether or not he should answer.

"Yes, I think that I am, but are you following him too and why did you come to Paris?" Harris leaned toward Marie, waiting for her answer.

"To be honest, Mr. Harris, I'm not sure what I'm doing. My divorce was finalized this week. I hate my job and I think the feeling is mutual. I also thought I'd be a sex symbol by the time I was forty." Marie gave a half-hearted smile. Harris barked with laughter. His legs stretched out in front of him as he held his sides. He wiped tears from the edge of his eyes.

"But why are you staying at that hotel? That's the same address you told me where he would be staying," Harris asked.

"I told my sister the address where the concierge at the Ritz was sending the man's package because I was sure that my sister couldn't find a hotel near there. I didn't realize it was a hotel. I guess he kind of inspired me to travel here." Marie shrugged her shoulders and looked up at the Tower. He raised one eyebrow, considering what she'd said.

"Wait! The packages! What do you think is in those packages?" Harris hopped from his seat. "We need to get back there before they arrive!" He immediately began walking down the path to the boulevard.

"What about my macaroon?" Marie followed after Harris.

A short time later, Marie entered the hotel, sweating and panting. Harris spoke rapidly in French to the front desk clerk. His hands waved in the air while he attempted to explain something to the cool woman behind the desk. She merely shrugged at him. They spoke back and forth for some time and Marie was sure that she'd heard him curse under his breath. After a while, Harris turned away from the front desk and walked over to Marie.

"So, am I to assume that we missed those packages? And I'm not getting my macaroon?" Marie followed Harris across the room to a small couch. He flopped down and she sat beside him.

"Yes, it turns out the gentleman arrived yesterday and retrieved his packages then." Harris crossed his arms and leaned back. He appeared to be pouting.

"You know, I wonder what the packages looked like. Why were there 'packages' and not just a package?" Marie thought aloud. Harris turned towards Marie. He stood up and walked back to the counter and spoke again with the woman. Then he returned to Marie.

"She said that there were three large boxes. She said that he told her they were framed Jazz Fest Posters for his collection." Harris translated what the woman said.

"Not a smallish box that one would put a Fabergé box in?" Marie asked with a bright smile. Harris released a low growl. He sat next to her again. He pulled his small notebook out and began to flip through the pages. "What do you think were in those large boxes?"

"The museum was missing three items from the Impressionist's room along with the Faberge box." Harris didn't look up from his notebook as he spoke.

"Well, perhaps he was just returning them to their spiritual home. You know, with Paris being at the heart of the Impressionist movement," Marie joked. Harris was not happy. Marie looked around the room when her eyes fell on the large abstract painting on one wall. Marie whispered: "Mr. Harris, do you think that that desk clerk might know our mystery man personally?"

"What makes you ask that?" Harris looked over the top of his glasses at her.

"Something about what she said to you. You say he told her that those packages were framed posters for his collection. Did he actually tell her those were for his collection or does she know that he has a collection?" Marie explained softly while she watched to see if the woman at the front desk could hear them. If she could, she didn't look up from her computer. Marie stood up and stretched and then walked to the front desk.

"Mademoiselle, si vous plait, do you know the name of the man—l'homme—that my friend over there asked you about earlier?" Marie hoped she made sense to the woman. The woman smiled and laughed.

"Oui. His name is Philip Augustus. He has his packages delivered here regularly because he travels so much. He is the friend of the night manager of this hotel." The woman returned to typing on her computer.

"Is the manager here today?" Marie leaned forward. Harris joined Marie at the counter. Both waited for the woman to answer. She looked back at the two of them, her eyes darting between them. Marie nudged Harris lightly with her elbow. The man was being too intense.

"Non, he will not be back until tomorrow night—demain. I am not sure. He may return tonight. I do not know for sure. Your rooms will be ready this afternoon. I must return to my work now." The woman dismissed the two. From her expression, Marie doubted the woman would answer another question from the strange pair.

Marie looked down at her watch. It was not even ten yet. "I

could really use a macaroon and a gallon of coffee right about now; how about you, Harris?"

The two meandered a few blocks down the street to the Bon Marché. The department store was amazing. Marie drifted immediately to a bread counter with Harris trailing behind her. She pointed and gestured until the person behind the glass handed her some delightfully flakey bread and a macaroon. They then pointed her to another counter where they were making coffee.

She paid for her treats and coffee and found a small table with two chairs. She took a breath and shoved the whole macaroon in her mouth. It was raspberry and it was heaven.

Harris placed his cup and a huge baguette on the table. He tore off a piece of the bread, smeared some sort of spread on it, and ate. The two sat in silence for a while, just chewing. Marie watched shoppers walking past with their purchases. Why was it that everyone in Paris looked so fashionable?

"What do you think we should do next? I'm sure we can find the owner online..." Harris pulled his phone from his pocket and started typing. Marie chewed slowly.

"We? Am I playing detective now?" Marie asked, sipping the warm ambrosia disguised as coffee. Harris pulled off his glasses and pinched the top of his nose.

"Ms. Clyde, I'm sorry I said that yesterday. Would you like to continue playing detective with me? I think that you have very good instincts and—let's face it—I'm pretty sure you're enjoying this." Harris smiled at Marie. *He really is quite handsome*, Marie thought.

"Okay, I'll play detective with you, Mr. Harris. Can I try your baguette?" Marie reached over and tore off a piece of the bread and popped it into her mouth, "I've been thinking. While we're waiting for the owner of the hotel, maybe we can look at this from some different angles." Marie was getting excited. Harris raised an eyebrow, inviting her to continue, "Like, what do we know about the items that were stolen? Besides the Fabergé box, what paintings were stolen? Maybe if we figure out who wants them, then we can find them there."

"First of all, my name is Donald. May I call you Marie?" Harris asked and Marie nodded yes. "To answer your question, the three other items were a Cassatt, a Dégas and a Renoir. There could be hundreds or thousands of people who want them. Why do you enjoy going to the New Orleans Museum of Art to look at the Milton Fabergé Box? Wouldn't you want it?" Marie wiped her mouth with a napkin.

"I guess you're right, but don't you have a list of people who might be interested in illegally obtaining artwork?" Marie crumpled the napkin in her hand. Harris laughed.

"If I knew who those folks were, I'd have arrested them when I was in the FBI. My job is more interested in the return of the items than with who wanted to take them, but I see your point." Harris tapped the side of his coffee cup and took a sip.

"Maybe we could figure out who collects them here in Paris and see if they know this first King of France or the last King of the Franks." Marie tossed another bite of baguette in her mouth and contemplated getting another macaroon. Perhaps she should try the blue one this time?

"What do you mean, the last King of the Franks?" Harris leaned forward. He pulled out his notebook and read.

"That ridiculous name, Philip Augustus. Philip the Second of France was also known as Philip Augustus. He was the first king of France, last king of the Franks. Doesn't anybody read books or pay attention to European History? I might have also looked it up quickly on Wikipedia before we left the hotel." Marie smiled in triumph. She carefully dabbed the sides of her lips with a napkin, discovering a broken piece of macaroon at the corner of her lips. She popped the piece in her mouth. Harris raised an eyebrow at her.

"Marie, you are a remarkable and intelligent woman. Since we still have hours before our rooms are ready, how would you like to accompany me to Musée d'Orsay? I believe there are a few galleries and collectors around there. Maybe I can ask if any of them work with an art dealer named Philip Augustus." He reached his hand across the table. Marie examined his hand and hesitated. Should she take it? She reached out and took his hand. He held her hand tightly. The blue macaroon would have to wait.

Chapter 13

Paul arrived at the small gallery. The tiny shop was nestled between an equally small bar with an excellent aperitif and an antique shop with a front window that displayed a dusty framed poster of a stained-glass window depicting the Battle of Bovines. Paul always smiled when he saw the display.

A bell chimed as Paul entered the gallery. He watched Emile lift a painting from its hook on the wall and draw it close under his nose. The slender man with a shock of white hair appeared to sniff the painting. Paul coughed, but Emile continued to sniff.

Emile pressed his thin lips together in disgust, leaning the painting against the wall beneath its spot on the wall. "I have been waiting all day to remove that miserable fake. Do you have the paintings?" Emile finally turned and stared at Paul through his wire-rimmed fake lenses.

"That is awfully rich coming from a man who five years ago couldn't tell the difference between a Picasso and a potato." A smile crept across Emile's lips.

"Oui, that was before I developed taste—or at least a taste

for making money. Show me!" Paul crossed the small space and handed Emile the three boxes. The two headed to a windowless back room crowded with oil and pastel paintings of various sizes and styles leaning against the walls. A huge empty table dominated the middle of the room. Emile opened the boxes with a quick slice of a knife that he usually concealed on his waistband.

He placed each painting on the table and whistled. "This mother and child one is kind of cute, non?" Emile teased. The two men inspected the paintings.

"The buyer should be here tomorrow afternoon. Should I go ahead and hang them up?" Emile lifted the Degas and sniffed the painting. "See, this smells right—like money." Paul shook his head at his strange little clerk. Emile was perfect as the snooty gallery assistant, selling attractive artist reproductions of famous paintings along with other unknown artists' work. Rarely did anyone but a lost tourist enter the gallery and when he or she did, they would often marvel at the reproductions and ask to use the bathroom.

"Where will we display the Fabergé?" Emile asked as he leaned over the third painting.

"There was a problem with the Fabergé," Paul answered as he turned to leave. Emile shot straight up.

"What do you mean a problem?" Emile followed Paul into the main room. Emile rubbed the tips of his fingers together, awaiting Paul's response.

"Apparently, the buyer called in a second contractor. He got to it before I did, but I know where to find him." Paul grimaced, thinking about LaCroix. Through his contacts, he knew that LaCroix had checked into the George V. LaCroix was flashy, no panache. He probably didn't even know who George V was, just that the hotel was posh.

Paul looked down at his watch and calculated in his head. He had three days to retrieve the box from LaCroix and present it to the buyer. He assumed the rendezvous had not changed, but Paul's price for the box certainly had. "Emile, I need to make a call."

Paul stepped outside the store and stood on the deserted street. He pulled the burner phone from his pocket and began to dial the number he'd memorized after he'd received the strange email from the mysterious buyer. It was nothing but a picture of the Fabergé Box, a six-figure dollar amount, a question mark and a phone number.

He had called before he flew to New Orleans, confirming with the mechanical voice that he would do as promised and to have the money ready. The voice on the other line told him where and when they would rendezvous. He listened to the ringing on the line.

"Yes, Mr. Augustus? Did you have a good flight to Paris?" The robotic voice answered. Something was unnerving about hearing the voice say his name. *How did it know he was already in Paris?*

"You hired someone else to retrieve the box?" Paul asked. The line sounded like it went dead then crackled.

"Yes, a friend of yours," said the voice. "It seems that Mr. LaCroix has the box now. What do you plan to do about that? I only promised him half the amount I offered you." The voice taunted Paul. He ground his teeth in disgust. The voice continued: "What is the problem? Criminals are criminals. Who cares who gets the box?"

"I will get that box from LaCroix and the price will go up another hundred thousand!" Paul barked into the phone. He turned around on the street and looked around to ensure that no one could overhear him.

"Of course, you will because you are a criminal," the voice shot back and then offered a mechanical laugh. Paul felt heat rise in his face every time the voice called him a criminal, like it was angry with him. "I'll see LaCroix tomorrow evening at the hotel, unless you find him first. I tell you what—if you get the box back, I'll give you another hundred thousand, but I don't think that you can do it." Paul listened to the voice. Did the voice realize it had revealed his plan to Paul? Doubt crept up Paul's spine. He should just let the job go, but he couldn't stand not answering a challenge.

"When I have it, I'll contact you," Paul answered, enunciating each word. Again, the voice laughed a little. Paul ground his teeth and hung up. He looked down at his phone and realized that his hands were actually shaking.

He tapped in the number for the George V. He waited while the phone rang twice and a sweet voice answered in French. He asked to be connected to the room number he'd gotten from his contact. He drew in a deep breath.

"Hello?" An unsure familiar voice answered. Paul had not spoken to LaCroix in twenty years.

"Cross, it's Paul." Paul responded without greeting. He ground his teeth together.

"It's LaCroix. Eh, Pauly, long time no see." LaCroix sounded cheerful at first, but his voice had changed, "What do you want?"

"I heard you got the Milton Fabergé Box," Paul spoke automatically. He could hear LaCroix moving around. There was a rustling of sheets and a low murmuring in the background.

"Is that what it's called? I bet if I could pry those diamonds off it and sell them individually I'd be rich." LaCroix laughed into the phone. Paul could hear him whisper something to the other person in the room next to him. He could hear a shrill giggle in the background. Paul rubbed his temple, feeling a headache forming.

"Who hired you to steal it?" Paul tried to push the frustration from his voice. LaCroix made some sort of kissing sound over the phone. The woman replied something obscene in a strong British accent.

"What's it to you, Pauli? Why are you even calling? All you need to know is that I got it first and you didn't, did you? The buyer backed a winner and I'm reaping the rewards," LaCroix bragged into the phone. "Hey, you know, Tate is still pissed with you for taking those stones."

"So, you're still working for that piece of work?" Paul asked, ignoring LaCroix's other jabs.

"Not for long, not after this job…" The shrill woman's voice interrupted LaCroix. Paul couldn't hear what she was saying, but he knew it was something about Tate. Paul shook his head. "Sorry you missed your shot on the box, but what can I say? I guess I'm better than you." Paul heard the woman laugh and LaCroix hung up on Paul.

Paul put the phone in his pocket and entered the gallery. Emile had finished putting up the painting. The three pieces looked amazing on the wall. The two men examined the pieces closely, a Degas, a Renoir and a Cassatt.

Emile returned to the desk in the back of the gallery and picked up a desk calendar. He flipped through the pages. "The buyer for the Cassatt will come at eleven and the buyer for the Renoir and the Degas will come at noon. Amelie will arrive tomorrow to open the shop. I'll be running late, but I'll be here by 10:30, perhaps 10:45 at the latest," Emile explained. Paul nodded, knowing that Emile always ran late. Paul would be there before the buyers came.

Paul thought about tomorrow. Tomorrow would be busy. He had a Fabergé box to steal tomorrow.

Chapter 14

"Do you think that they sell crepes with just cheese?" Marie looked dreamily at the food cart along the banks of the Seine. She could smell a strong whiff of Nutella. Again her stomach rumbled.

Harris slowed his march and looked back at the dawdling Marie. She licked her lips, and as if pulled by a string, she approached the stand. "How can you possibly be hungry?" Harris asked.

A man handed Marie a toasty crepe and she handed him a couple of Euros, "Merci," she said, smiling and then turned to Harris, "I guess investigations in Paris make me hungry." She bit into the crepe.

"Investigations? You aren't investigating anything. I'm investigating. You're eating any item of food we pass." Harris stomped his foot. Marie swallowed her bite, wiping off a crumb with the back of her hand.

"I beg your pardon, sir. First of all, you wouldn't have known to look in Paris in the first place, if not for my going to the Ritz Carlton in New Orleans. Next, you wouldn't know the name of the man we're looking for if I hadn't asked at the hotel. I think that I'm pretty good at this investigating thing. I bet that I can find those paintings and the Fabergé Box before you can. We're in one of the culinary capitals of the world. It would be an insult to Paris not to experience all the delights it offers. You know, this is my vacation." Marie stomped her foot and took another bite of her crêpe. A cascade of crumbs fell on her blouse and she brushed them away. "Why would you have me come along with you to the Musée d'Orsay if not to help investigate? I can eat a crêpe and investigate. I can do both."

Harris took off his glasses and walked to the railing, looking out over the Seine. "I'm sorry. What I said was rude…" Harris let the sentence stop. Marie waited for the "but." She stood next to him and tried to see what he was looking at across the Seine.

"Aren't you going to add something? Say 'but'?" Marie tore another piece of the crepe with her teeth. She wondered if it would be considered piggish to buy another crepe as more crumbs fell on her. The cheese was incredible. She shut her eyes for a moment, just savoring it.

"No, I'm not." Harris pushed his glasses back up his nose, "I guess you aren't sharing any of that?" Marie tightened her grip on the crepe, squinting her eyes as if daring him to try and take it from her. She shook her head 'no'. He peered across the Seine. Something caught his attention. "Are you almost finished with that crepe?" Marie popped the last bite into her mouth and chewed quickly.

"What do you see?" Marie asked energized. Her gaze scanned the river, watching a tour boat slowly float past. Cars and bicycles hurried back and forth across the bridge. Staring at the bridge, she remembered an image from *Madeline*, the children's book, of a child walking along the railing. "Are you looking at the bridge? It kind of reminds me of the *Madeline* book."

Harris grimaced at Marie and then spoke: "No, I'm not looking at the bridge, I'm looking at the neighborhood across the river. As I recall, there are a ton of galleries there, maybe a hundred in five or ten square blocks. How can we narrow down where to look?" As if on cue, a raindrop splattered on the rail between the two.

They ran quickly to the corner and crossed the busy intersection, looking for shelter. Harris pointed to the entrance of a large hotel and the two stepped inside the lobby which was decorated in shiny brass and cream marble. They stood for a moment at the doorway looking out as the rain began to fall, watching pedestrians rushing along the sidewalks under a rainbow of umbrellas.

"I guess we'll have to wait it out." Marie sighed, leaning against a small plaque on the wall. She turned to read it. She expected it to offer some historical fact, but instead it proudly displayed the corporate logo of the company that owned the hotel brand. "Hey, I have an idea."

Harris continued to peer out at the rain, "What's your idea? And don't say let's go eat something."

"Okay, okay, I'm full for now anyway. Here's my idea and this might be a little convoluted, but here goes: we look up who or what corporation owns Hotel Marguerite and see if they own any other hotels around this area." Harris turned and stared at Marie.

"Why?" Harris pulled his phone from his pocket, ready to type.

"Because maybe that manager who knows our thief met our thief in the same neighborhood, this neighborhood. Maybe the manager works at a hotel property around here..." Marie's brown eyes widened as she got more animated. Harris found himself mesmerized for a moment and then shook his head.

"But we don't even know the manager's name or if he's there so we can speak with him…" Harris interrupted. Marie shook her head.

"We don't have to speak to him. We just look at galleries and shops that are near that hotel. Maybe we can find another clue." Marie was almost shouting, shaking with excitement. Harris shushed her.

"That would be a huge coincidence. He could be halfway to Geneva by now. The paintings and box could be in some dirty gas station or anywhere." Harris' shoulders slumped. Marie thought about his doubts.

"Yes, but what if we just took a risk? We could be wrong and then we can find somewhere else to eat." Marie smiled convincingly at Harris. Something about her expression inspired him. She reached out and patted his shoulder. For a moment they looked deeply into each other's eyes. She noticed the flecks of gray in the blue; even his eyes looked strong.

Harris leaned a little forward and then abruptly stood up straight, "Great idea; let me look that up and we can narrow down our search." He cleared his throat. Marie rolled her eyes and returned to leaning against the plaque, watching the passing traffic. Harris tapped silently on his phone.

"Okay, I think I have a lead. Hotel Marguerite is owned with three other properties, one is about six blocks from Hotel Marguerite. One is in Montmartre. The fourth is about six blocks from here, on the other side of the river." He handed Marie his phone so she could see the picture.

"It looks like the rain is letting up, let's go for it." Marie handed back his phone, pushing open the glass door of the hotel.

After two and a half hours of visiting fifteen galleries in a ten block radius from the hotel, Marie was ready to quit. If she saw one more lousy painting of the Eiffel Tower in the rain, she might puke. Her feet ached, her clothing soaked, and jetlag had finally caught up with her. Marie read the time on her watch twice. Surely now her room would be ready.

Harris, on the other hand, appeared energized by the search. His speed seemed to increase as they got closer to the last gallery on the list. Marie lagged behind him, wondering why she ever thought aiding in the investigation of an art theft would be fun. *Yes, I regret this choice*, Marie thought. *I should be passed out in my hotel room, dreaming about croissants.*

Harris reached the glass front door of the small shop and stopped. Marie arrived and read the sign: "Fermé". Harris tried to peer through the glass, but the shades were drawn. Marie blew out a long held sigh.

"They don't re-open until tomorrow at 10 a.m. I didn't realize how late it had gotten." Harris looked down at his watch. The street was quiet. Marie looked left and right, realizing that she wasn't sure which way she should go to return to the hotel. Harris paced in front of the store.

"Mr. Harris, I think that we need to call it a day and admit defeat," Marie spoke quietly. Harris frowned and kept pacing. He stood in front of the antique store next to the shop and admired himself in the front window, sweeping his palm through his hair. Marie stood next to him and almost shrieked at her reflection—brown frizzy hairs framed her head like small lightning bolts.

"The Battle of Bovines? Ms. Clyde, you read a lot. Are you familiar with this battle? Have you ever heard of it?" Marie tried to read the writing on the bottom of the poster in the window. All she could understand was that the stained glass window depicted the Battle of Bovines. Marie shook her head.

"I read some history, but I'm not familiar with that battle. I wonder if it was part of the Hundreds Year War or something like that. I'll look it up," Marie offered cheerfully. She pulled out her cellphone, typed in the name and began reading an article about the battle.

"I think you might be too reliant on Wikipedia. You know that they aren't always accurate," Harris said while Marie began to read aloud.

"And I quote: 'The final battle of the Anglo-French War of 1213 to 1214.' Geez, I wonder how many of these wars they must have had '...took place July 27, 1214 near Bovines in Flanders. Holy Roman Emperor Otto the Fourth...'" She stopped abruptly, her eyes growing larger as she read silently.

"What? What happened to Otto?" Harris asked, leaning over Marie's shoulder.

"We found him! Philip Augustus fought in the Battle of Bovines. This cannot be a coincidence." Marie felt exuberant.

Harris shook his head. "Maybe, but it could just be coincidence." Marie pulled on the front door of the gallery, somehow hoping the door was unlocked but it wasn't. Harris pulled out his phone and began to furiously type, while marching down the street.

Marie followed him. "What do we do now?" He seemed a million miles away, almost halfway down the block.

"We go back to the hotel and take a nap." When he reached the end of the block, he waved for a taxi. One stopped at the curb and he held the door, waiting for Marie.

Marie thought she'd just sleep for a quick two hour nap. Instead she awoke at 2 a.m., still wearing her shoes and her purse strap crossed over her chest. The bedside lamp was still on. *Had she not moved from that position all afternoon and night?*

She padded to her bathroom and brushed her teeth. She stripped down and returned to the bed. She pulled the covers to her chin and turned out the light, hoping that sleep would overtake her, but she was up at 2 a.m.

Lying in the dark, she wondered when the last time was that she'd stayed up this late. Was she in college? Probably. She turned over, trying to clear her mind. She felt like she could run a marathon.

Where had that thought emerged? She would never want to run a marathon, but she was wide awake. What could she do now? What should she do at 2 a.m. in Paris? Perhaps go on a walk? Was that safe in Paris?

Marie sat up and switched on the light. It was no use pretending to sleep. She wasn't sleepy now. Maybe she should take a walk, wander near the Eiffel Tower again. Didn't it light up at night? Would it still be lighting up at 2 in the morning? Marie turned off the light again and flopped back on the pillow.

She willed her eyes shut. Thoughts invaded her attempt at rest. She wondered what Michael thought about their divorce. Was he happy now with whatever the woman's name was? Marie turned on her side.

Did the restructuring at work mean she was getting fired? Restructuring usually meant people got fired. David did seem to have it in for her. Marie turned on her other side. Her brain quieted for a moment.

What was she going to do with her life? What was the point? Marie's eyes popped open. Was she really having an existential crisis at 2 a.m. in Paris? That made sense. Or perhaps all existential crises were actually caused by jet lag. That made more sense. Marie turned on the bedside lamp.

Marie slipped on her clothes, ran a brush through her hair and quietly left her room. She decided to take the stairs because it seemed quieter in the darkened building. The stairwell was lighted by small wall sconces that turned on as she got closer. When she finally arrived at the door to the lobby, she paused and listened at the door. Through the square window, she could see the back of two men seated in the lobby at small table, two half-filled glasses and a bottle of wine between them.

"It was a good trip, Jean. Thank you for holding onto my packages. I just don't feel comfortable sending them to the gallery if there isn't someone there." Marie recognized the voice. It was her mystery man.

"It was no problem. What did you see while you were there? I hear New Orleans is very exciting." The other voice replied and the gentleman sipped his wine. Marie stepped back from the door. She should tell Harris, but she had no idea what room he was in and she couldn't ask because there was no other route to the front desk except through the lobby.

Should she go back upstairs? Should she try to sneak into the lobby? Did she have Harris' number? She started to dig through her purse to find his card.

"Will we see you at the show this week? I know how you love antiques. Lots of Nouveau style." The two men were now standing. Paul faced the door and Marie ducked down, hoping he hadn't seen her. She could hear Paul bid the man goodbye and the opening and shutting of the electric sliding doors.

Marie pushed open the stairwell door. The other man turned to face her with a smile on his face. She read the nametag pinned to his blazer. He quickly picked up the two glasses and wine bottle from the table. "Bonjour, Madame, may I help you?"

"The man who was just here. Where did he go?" The man in

the blazer wrinkled his brow, considering her question.

"What man, Madame? It is very late. Do you need something? Perhaps a glass of wine to help rest?" He lifted the bottle and glasses while raising his eyebrows in an offering to Marie.

"No, thank you, but there was a man just here with you. Where did he go? I heard you while I was coming down the steps." Marie moved to step around him but he moved to block her. She zigged and he zagged and she stepped through the sliding doors onto the quiet street. No one was there. A chill cut through her in the dark and she stepped back inside.

The man in the blazer was now behind the front desk, placing the bottle behind him. Marie smiled at him and looked at the stand of maps and brochures next to the desk. Frustration built inside her.

"You had two glasses of wine. I know you didn't drink both. The man who was with you—I've met him before. Was it Philip Augustus? Paul?" The clerk dropped his arms to his sides, his warm expression gone.

"You are the second person who's asked after my friend today? What do you want with him?" A chill ran down Marie's spine as she stepped back from the desk.

"I just feel certain that I've met him before. He kissed me," Marie blurted out before she could stop herself. The man behind the desk smiled and tsk-tsked. Marie shrugged and smiled back. She moved toward the front door.

"Where are you going so late, Madame?" Marie pivoted back and tugged on her purse's strap.

"I thought maybe a walk would help me sleep." Marie answered weakly. Again the man tsk-tsked.

"No, no, it's late and dangerous for a woman alone in Paris. Let me offer you a glass of wine." While he might have meant what he said as a warning, it felt much more like a threat. He immediately came around the desk and walked to the other side of the lobby. He entered the kitchen area and emerged with a glass of wine for Marie. She thanked him as he handed it to her. He stood before her as she sipped.

"Merci. I will head back to bed. Thank you." Marie and the man walked to the elevator and she stepped inside. As she closed the door, he stood on the other side looking at her through the small window. Maybe the wine would help her sleep, but she doubted it.

Marie awoke at ten and rushed down the stairs. A few people were seated at the tables in the lobby enjoying a breakfast. Marie scanned the room looking for Harris. She needed to speak to him. Where was he? Was he still in his room?

Marie approached the front desk. This time a skinny young man with a goatee greeted her. She asked to be connected to Harris' room. She looked longingly at the guests finishing breakfast. The same fashionable woman from the night before carried a bowl of fruit and set it on the buffet. The young man dialed the number and handed her the receiver. Marie listened to about six rings and decided to head out. She handed the receiver to the man and thanked him. She would return to the store from yesterday and look for herself. She considered grabbing a healthy piece of fruit but instead she snatched a pain au chocolat from the buffet and left.

Marie tried to remember the path the two had taken yesterday. Twice she found herself heading down the wrong street and backtracking. At last she found the tiny street. As she walked closer, she noticed two police cars parked along the curb outside the gallery. Officers milled back and forth in front.

When she arrived at the front door of the small store, she could hear Harris from inside the gallery. He barked some type of order in French. She attempted to enter the front door and find Harris. A policeman angrily ran toward her waving his arms. She stepped back. Harris followed the officer and said something quickly in French.

"What are you doing here, Ms. Clyde?" Marie noticed the formality had returned to their exchanges. Harris stood in the doorway, blocking Marie's view. Marie tried to look around him. Behind him, a young woman sniffled and cried. She was seated on a stool inside, speaking with a police officer. Marie could see another officer wearing white gloves holding a canvas and carrying it across the room to the third officer.

"You found the artwork? The paintings were here? The Fabergé?" Marie asked excitedly. Harris turned his head slightly and shouted something to the three officers. All of them stopped what they were doing and nodded.

Harris released a sigh and cocked his head to the side, "Yes, we found the three paintings, but we haven't yet recovered the Milton Fabergé Box. Mr. Augustus is not here, but he's the Paris police department's problem, not mine. What are you doing here?" Harris asked again.

"I wanted to talk to you. I saw him last night at the hotel. I thought we'd go here together today." Marie spoke breathlessly. She felt disappointed and left out. An officer carried one of the pieces, covered in a white cloth, through the front door to a waiting van.

"Ms. Clyde, you have been incredibly helpful in finding this place. Thank you. I will be handling the rest of this investigation." Harris squinted and nodded at her, as if channeling Clint Eastwood. With that, she was dismissed. He returned to the other officer in the gallery.

Marie looked back and forth along the street and noticed a café next door. She went in and tried to find a place to stop and think. Harris' dismissal stung. Didn't she help him figure out where her mystery man was and the gallery? He thought she had good instincts and was smart, but now she was off the investigation. She laughed to herself, thinking about the term "off the investigation" like she was a detective or something.

The bar was cozy—dark wood with black and white framed photographs on the wall. Marie rehearsed asking for a glass of wine in her head as she approached the counter. At the bar, she saw the chiseled profile of her mystery man. His eyes were downcast, reading a thick volume on the bar and half glass of red wine next to the book. Marie cleared her throat and stood up straighter. She was here, in Paris with her mystery man just a few steps away.

She wracked her brain with what to say. Would he even recognize her? Or even care? Marie looked down at her blouse, covered in crumbs. She wiped them away and walked over and sat on the stool next to him.

"In all the gin joints, in all the world… I think that's how the phrase starts." Marie whispered the words with a small laugh. He only heard the laugh and turned towards Marie. His beautiful clear eyes widened in recognition.

"I didn't hear what you said, but somehow I'm sure it really was humorous. It is Marie, isn't it? What are you doing here?" Paul closed the book and signaled the bartender who promptly placed a glass of wine in front of Marie. All she could do was smile. He'd remembered who she was.

"Hello, Paul." Marie giggled again. He smiled at her, but the expression was strained.

"You know my name," Paul spoke aloud, but almost as if speaking to himself. She noticed him clenching his jaw.

"Yes, you told me your name at the museum." Marie reminded him. She followed his gaze through the front window of the bar. One of the police cars drove away. Marie studied his profile.

Marie was mesmerized and then reality began to hit her. *Was this man a thief? Was she actually sitting right next to an international art thief?*

"Hello." He raised his perfect brown brows, "It is Marie? Marie. Hello, I am surprised to see you here. Why are you here?" Paul took a sip of his wine. Marie took a gulp of her wine.

"I wanted to speak with you. No, that isn't it, I came to Paris because…" Marie took another gulp and finished her wine. Again Paul's eyes widened at this wild woman next to him. "I am sorry, what was your question again?" Paul opened his mouth and Marie raised her hand to stop him. "Yes, why am I here? That is a good question. You and I met on a really bad day for me and you kissed me."

"You came here because of a kiss?" Paul lifted an eyebrow and took another sip. A smug expression settled on his face. He rested his elbow on the bar and rested his cheek against his fist. He looked over Marie's shoulder. Marie turned and saw Harris walk past with a police officer. She pressed her lips together in frustration.

"No, not just because of kiss. Well, maybe a little, but I wanted to know why you kissed me." Paul looked distracted. Again he signaled the bartender, this time for the check. He rolled his eyes and began to stand. Marie grabbed his arm: "Did you kiss me to distract me from what you were doing in the control room at the Museum? Did you steal the Milton Fabergé Box and those Impressionists paintings? Or is this all a coincidence?"

Paul froze and sat down in the stool. He swiveled her stool so she looked right at him, gripping her upper arms. "What are you doing here, Marie? Do you work with that investigator? Are you working with LaCroix and Tate? What is your game? I should have known that sad sack story and fall were the work of a consummate professional."

Marie's expression was blank. "What are you talking about?" Paul gripped tighter and leaned closer. He shook her. Marie winced and Paul let go and leaned back in his chair.

"Are you working for the buyer? Checking up on me? You know I didn't get the Fabergé and LaCroix did. Who are you?" Paul whispered and looked over his shoulder. The room was almost empty but for a grey moustached man reading a newspaper at one table and another patron arguing with the bartender at the end of the bar.

Marie rubbed her arms, "First of all, no one has ever called me a professional, but I digress. Second, I am not a sad sack. Thirdly, you really are a thief." The realization lodged in Marie's chest. *Paul was not some sophisticated playboy. He was an actual thief!* Marie swallowed. Was she in danger sitting here with him? His expression hardened as he crossed his arms.

Marie mirrored his posture, trying to project calm: "So, you stole those paintings from the New Orleans Museum of Art, but you didn't steal the Fabergé Box?" Paul pursed his lips. "This LaCroix has the box. And you think that I work for…" Marie let the sentence drop, waiting for Paul's reply. His expression was blank. "I work at a non-profit assisting the editor of publications and doing research."

"How did you find me?" Paul asked, again looking over his shoulder.

"I'm good at research. I read. I listen," Marie answered.

"And you were able to track me here? Because of a kiss?" Paul asked incredulously. He shook his head. Marie shrugged and tried to smile, but somehow it looked more like a grimace.

"It was a good kiss." Marie laughed as she spoke. Paul laughed as well. The tension between them seemed to evaporate, but he still glanced over her shoulder. "Why? Why did you kiss me?"

"I don't know. Perhaps I thought an interesting woman like you needed to remember that." Paul stood up to leave.

"Wait, where are you going?" Marie tugged the wool sleeve of his sweater. He looked down at her hand and she snatched it away. He nodded his head toward the commotion happening outside.

"I have an errand, but maybe we can meet at the George V for a drink this evening." Marie wanted to ask him more questions, but he smiled down at her. "Look, I really need to go. We can meet there about eight and you can ask all the questions you want. I like curious women." He leaned toward her, tipped her chin upward, and kissed her softly on her lips. Before Marie could open her eyes, Paul was halfway out the back door of the bar. She touched her warm lips and sighed.

"Who was that? Were you kissing that thief?" Harris exclaimed from the doorway of the bar. Marie swung around on her stool. Her cheeks were bright red. The other patrons in the bar looked between Harris and Marie.

"Well…" Marie squeaked out and shrugged. Harris raced past her to the back door of the bar. He immediately marched to the counter and grabbed Marie by the shoulders, facing her toward him.

"What were you doing?" Marie's eyes widened and she swallowed hard. Harris loosened his grip on her shoulders, stepping back. He took off his glasses and furiously wiped them with a handkerchief in his back pocket.

"You might break those if you wipe any harder." Marie offered with a weak smile. Harris squinted at Marie. "To answer your question, yes, he did kiss me. Yes, he is the thief, but he didn't steal the Fabergé Box," Marie blurted out the last part while Harris put on his glasses.

"You kissed that guy? Are you kidding me?" Harris looked at the ceiling and shook his head.

"He kissed me." Marie defended herself. *Why did he care? She was just "Ms. Clyde" to him.*

"It didn't look like you were putting up much of a defense. I cannot believe you. That guy is a thief. You could do so much better than him. Unbelievable! At least I finally have a picture of what he looks like." Harris pulled his phone from his pocket and showed Marie the screen. The picture was through the glass door of a suave Paul leaning down toward Marie with her ponytail coming undone.

"It's a good picture," Marie said softly. Harris yanked the phone away and put it in his pocket. He began to walk to the door and turned around as if to say something to Marie, but instead he shook a finger at her. "I guess I'll see you at the hotel?" Marie said as the door closed behind him.

Chapter 15

Marie wandered the streets of Paris in a daze. She made her way to the Boulevard Saint Germain, peeking in shop windows and stopping at small cafes. She weaved through the neighborhoods, trying to get lost, when she finally found a small park, in the shadow of the Bon Marché that she'd visited the day before. She sat on a bench across from a carousel and just watched the horses rise and fall to some tinkling tune she couldn't identify.

A wave of weariness swept over her and she felt the familiar tears well up in her eyes. She was in one of the most beautiful cities in all of the world and she was sitting on a bench feeling sorry for herself. Was being here in Paris really going to change her life? Would she suddenly find herself filled with confidence and ready to pursue her dreams? Did she even know what those dreams were?

A small red ball rolled toward her feet, shaking Marie from her thoughts. A young boy ran toward the bench and stood nervously before her, his small palms outstretched. Marie smiled at him and leaned down to pick up the ball, admiring its ruby red color. Handing the ball to the child, she stood up. *Who was LaCroix?* she wondered. *He had the Fabergé box.*

Marie gathered her belongings from the bench and quickly exited the park. She headed down the street to her hotel. She needed a computer and she needed to speak with Harris.

Paul strolled into the lobby of the George V. The space was pristine, glistening white and brimming with fresh flowers. Businessmen and women wandered about the lobby, chatting with each other or speaking on their phones. He moved quickly to the elevators and entered one, pressing the button.

The doors opened to a beige and wood paneled hallway. Paul padded silently down the hallway to the room and opened the door with this key card. He shut the door behind him and immediately went to the window, opening the curtains and then the window. He looked out over the ledge to the street below. He could hear the horns from cars, but as evening approached no one on the street below was looking up.

Carefully he stepped through the window, touching the ledge with his toe and then planting his foot. He stood on the ledge, facing the building, for a moment and sighed. Slowly he shuffled along the edge to the next window, stopping for a moment to check the street below, and then continuing until he stood next to LaCroix's window.

Paul listened. LaCroix was practically shouting. It sounded like one side of a conversation. "Yea, I got it...The hotel's good—real nice, real classy...So I meet the buyer when...Look, boss, I'm the one taking this risk here...What do I mean? I mean that I need more money for this..." LaCroix sounded full of bravado and then he gulped and got quieter, "Oh, you're here..."

Paul was reaching for the latch on the window when he

heard a crash and thud come from the room. He snatched back his hand and flattened himself against the stone façade of the building. He leaned his head towards the window, straining to hear the voices coming from the room.

"Son of a...!" A cracking sound stopped the speaker, LaCroix, from finishing his curse. Paul heard LaCroix groan. He could hear the voice of a woman, but he couldn't make out what she was saying. She was speaking slowly.

"Look, here it is...Take it...What are you doing? I don't know her. I don't know what you're talking about. I don't remember anything. I didn't really know her. Please, I'm sorry..." LaCroix begged. Again, another cracking sound came from the room and LaCroix moaned again. Paul heard the woman laugh. A chill shot down Paul's spine.

"What do you want me to say? I'll say anything! Please don't kill me...." Then the woman asked LaCroix something and he responded, "Yeah, Paul, I mean, I don't know. You got the wrong guy. I didn't do anything..." Paul heard a familiar sound. He knew what a bullet sounded like.

Another voice gruffly spoke, "We need to go now." Paul slid carefully to the window just in time to see the door shutting behind two figures. The room was dark, but Paul could see the furniture and other items tossed about. He opened the latch and climbed over the sill.

In the darkness, he could hear panting and he smelled smoke and something floral. Paul righted a lamp on the table and turned it on. LaCroix lay on a Persian rug, his hands covering a wound on his chest. Paul rushed to his side, glancing around the room for a cloth to stop the bleeding. He found a small blanket on a chair and pressed it to LaCroix's chest. LaCroix fluttered his eyes and opened them. His gaze focused on Paul. The injured man tried to speak.

"Cross, what did you get yourself into? Hang on, I'll get help." Paul scanned the room looking for the telephone. He began to stand to reach for the receiver, but LaCroix gripped Paul's wrist, covering it with blood. LaCroix shook his head and tried to form words. No noise would come out, so Paul leaned his ear to LaCroix's mouth.

LaCroix coughed and sputtered and whispered, "Her mother." He hissed out the last words before suddenly going still. Paul leaned back from LaCroix and looked down at the cloth he held over LaCroix's chest. It was soaked through. LaCroix's eyes remained open, seemingly staring vacantly at some point on the ceiling. LaCroix was gone.

Paul stood up, trembling. He looked down at his suit, blood splattered on his sleeves and shirt, and his hands red. He wiped his hands on the legs of his pants, trying to clean them. He breathed in and out. As he scanned the room, his eyes fell on a large black velvet bag near the pillow on the bed. He carefully stepped around LaCroix and picked up the bag, immediately realizing what was inside.

He heard a pounding on the door and a demand in French for the door to be opened. Paul ran to the open window and climbed over the sill, pulling the curtains and window closed behind him. He didn't bother to look down as he inched along the ledge to the window of his room.

He climbed into his room and released a sigh. He looked down and could see a police car pulling up in front of the hotel. He needed to get out of there.

Her afternoon research resulted in zilch as she tried to determine who LaCroix might possibly be. She had clicked through articles about the theft at the museum and was surprised to discover more information about the family who'd loaned the

Fabergé Box to the museum twenty years ago. The news story included a romantic piece about the box being a gift to the family's matriarch from a European count of dubious origin. The count, historians had discovered, was the former coachman to the real count who had used the actual count's credentials to enter high society and purchase the box using the real count's account. The true count, unfortunately, died of typhus before anyone discovered the purchase and its subsequent gifting to Mrs. Charles Milton, Sr. during the 1930s. Mrs. Milton, believing her count was dead, returned to New Orleans and married Mr. Milton. At her death, she then gifted the Fabergé Box to the youngest daughter of the family, who in turn, loaned it to the museum in the late 1990s. Marie smiled at the story but she was still filled with questions. Frustrated, she discovered that it was already 6:45 p.m. so she decided she needed to get ready to head to the George V.

Marie arrived at the George V around 7:10. As she approached the entrance, she noticed a small group of British tourists. A squat man in a shiny suit was arguing into a cellphone and a young woman in a skin tight leopard print dress was tapping her pointy toed shoe impatiently. The two strode into the lobby after the short man shoved the doorman. Marie hung back, waiting for the two ruffians to either move along or go inside first.

Marie entered the hotel. She was early, but she wanted to look around. She'd read about the famous hotel and was enjoying the lobby as she kept her eyes open for Le Bar. In the lobby, dozens of columns were positioned around the edges. Flower decorations topped them all. She stopped and admired one arrangement while people milled around her.

Everyone looked so fashionable, even more so than at her hotel. Women and men wore sleek dark suits that seemed to fit them perfectly. Each woman appeared to have every hair held tightly in place in buns and understated makeup. The men looked like they'd just showered at the gym. Marie sighed heavily to herself.

She looked down at her black dress and pink scarf, tugging at the ends of the scarf. She patted the dress, hoping it didn't have too much lint on it or too many wrinkles. She continued to watch the crowd, looking for Paul. A few tourists walked in, chattering loudly on their way to the marble front desk. At one point, she thought she saw someone she recognized, a huge man stuffed into a brown suit, but she shook her head, reminding herself that she was in Paris, and didn't really know anyone here.

Marie looked down at her watch; twenty minutes had passed. She was going to ask at the front desk for directions to the bar, when she heard pounding footsteps run through the front doors of the George V. Marie turned and watched as a man from behind the front desk ran to greet the three police officers and lead them towards a bank of elevators. Marie walked to the front desk when she felt arms wrap around her midsection.

She could feel someone breathing in her ear. She stiffened and he held her tightly. "Look, I'm sorry to do this to you, Marie. You seem really nice. I'm going to give you something and I need you to take it with you. Give it to my friend at the Hotel Marguerite. When I turn you around, please don't freak out." Marie recognized Paul's voice and slowly he released her from his grip. Marie turned slowly and saw why Paul would think she would freak out.

"Is that blood on you?" Marie asked quietly, her eyes widening. He pulled her close to him in an embrace. Marie struggled to free herself from him. "Let me go."

"I said, 'Don't freak out.' You have to believe me that I

didn't do anything." He sounded desperate as he spoke into her ear. Anyone around them would think that they were a couple sharing some intimate moment. More police officers poured into the lobby.

He pulled Marie with him to a corridor which led to the bar. He handed her a small black velvet bag. When she held it, she noticed that it felt heavier than she expected. Curious, she began to pull the strings on the bag open.

"Don't open it here. Just put it in your purse," he hissed at Marie as they moved quickly down the hallway. A police officer headed towards them and again, Paul pulled Marie into an embrace, nuzzling her ear so the officer couldn't see his face.

"Hey, stop that." The officer passed them and Marie pushed him away. "What's going on? Why do you have blood on you? What is in this bag?"

"Just put it in your purse, have a drink at the bar and go back to the Hotel Marguerite. I didn't kill LaCroix. There was someone else there. Please just take it and go." Paul's eyes pleaded with Marie. Carefully she stuffed the item into her purse. Before she could look up from her purse, Paul vanished. Another police officer walked down the hallway.

Marie saw a sign for the Ladies' Room and entered it. Finding a stall, she shut the door behind her and hung her purse on the hook on the door. Gingerly she pulled the black bag from her purse and untied the strings, keeping the bag closed. She pulled apart the opening and gasped. She held a red enameled rectangular box surrounded by a band of one carat diamonds— the Milton Fabergé Box.

She immediately pulled the drawstrings on the bag closed and slapped a hand over her mouth. Then, slowly she opened the bag again and pulled the box from the bag, feeling its weight in her hands. She opened it and looked inside, marveling as she touched the soft velvet. Marie noticed the box exuded a light lavender scent. She snapped the box shut and slipped it back into the black bag and carefully put it in her purse.

Marie leaned on one wall of the stall and released a long breath. She needed to get to Harris. He'd know what to do. She unlocked the door and exited the stall. She needed to get back to the Hotel Marguerite quickly. She needed to get the box to Harris before Paul came to retrieve the box.

The lobby was now filled with police officers. They stopped people, asking for identification. A police woman approached Marie and spoke something to her and then repeated it in English, "May I see your identification, your passport, please?"

Marie nodded and reached into her purse, trying to avoid touching the bag. She pulled her passport from her purse and handed it to the woman. While the woman inspected it, Marie asked "What's happening?"

The officer looked from side to side and spoke softly, "A man was killed in his room tonight. Looks like a robbery."

"How terrible!" Marie murmured as her heart started to pound. The officer returned her passport and turned to the next person in the lobby, demanding his identification. Slowly, Marie walked to the front doors. A doorman held one open for her as she stepped through and walked quickly down the block, unsure where she was headed.

Marie hurried through the streets of Paris, clutching her purse tightly. She kept looking over her shoulder. She felt as if a shadow was following her from the fashionable hotel. She headed for busier streets and tried to stay close to the crowds.

At last, she stood at the front doors of the Hotel Marguerite. They slid open. Marie bolted through the doors and looked back, peering into the darkened street. She was sure someone was behind her, but no one was there.

"Madame, are you well?" Marie swung around and saw Jean, the night manager standing behind the front desk. "Is everything okay?" he inquired, leaning across the desk and looking towards the door.

"I thought someone was behind me," Marie answered breathlessly. She gripped the strap of her purse and shifted it to her other shoulder. The weight of the tiny box felt like a brick.

"You must be careful in Paris. There are pickpockets," the man offered and then returned to typing on his computer. Marie approached the desk.

"Would you please call Mr. Harris' room?" Marie asked. The man nodded and lifted the receiver of the phone. She could hear the odd buzzing or ringing and a familiar gruff voice answered in French. He handed the receiver to Marie.

"Donald, this is Marie. I need you to either come down here immediately or I need to see you right now." Marie exclaimed into the phone. She watched the night manager smile and turn away from the desk, busying himself elsewhere.

"Slow down, Marie. What's going on?" Harris asked with the same gruffness he used with the night manager.

"Please, Donald, I need to talk to you now. May I come to your room?" Marie pleaded. She heard him sigh heavily.

"Okay, Room 204." He clicked off and Marie handed the receiver to the night manager and ran to the stairs, taking them two at a time. She arrived at his door and tapped softly on the door.

When he opened the door, she tumbled forward into him. She hadn't realized she was actually leaning on the door while knocking. He caught her in his arms and righted her, closing the door behind her. He held her arms a little longer than necessary and looked down in her eyes. Finally, he dropped his hands to his sides and stepped back.

"So, what was so important that you needed to speak with me?" Harris walked over to the mini-fridge and opened it, pulling out a small bottle of white wine. He took two glasses from above the fridge and filled both glasses. He handed one to Marie, and Marie gladly took the glass and downed the Pinot Grigio. Harris blinked at her, slowly raising the glass to his lips and sipping.

"I saw Paul tonight. He gave me this." Marie placed her drink on the nearest table and sat on the corner of the bed. She opened her purse and pulled out the black velvet bag. Carefully she untied the drawstrings and opened the bag revealing the red Milton Fabergé Box.

"Oh, dear Lord!" Harris gulped his wine down and immediately poured another. She held out the box to him. He gulped down the second glass and put down his drink, wiping off his hands on his slacks. He reached for the box and took it from Marie. He drew it close to his face and inspected it, turning it over and opening it and closing it. "Please tell me again how this box came into your possession."

"I went to the George V to meet Paul at Le Bar. He came up to me and handed me the box. He told me to return to the hotel with it," Marie spoke softly. Harris sat close to her on the bed, his thigh pressing against her. He continued examining the box.

"It looks like there's no damage to it. The museum will be thrilled to get this back." Harris smiled and put the box back in the velvet bag. "Why do I have a feeling there's something more to this story than you're telling me?"

"May I have another glass of wine?" Marie wrinkled her brow and handed him her glass. He quickly refilled it and returned to his spot next to her. She sipped her wine. She was now trembling as she placed the glass down. "Yes, there is something more. When Paul handed me the box, there was blood on him. He said he didn't kill LaCroix, but there was blood. I also think someone followed me here." Marie began to breathe in and out.

Harris put the box on the night table and pulled Marie into an embrace, holding her to his chest. She pressed into him, breathing in the scent of his aftershave and listened to his strong heartbeat. Marie's breath hitched and tears rolled down her cheeks.

Harris tilted Marie's chin so that he could look her in the eye. His warm thumb wiped tears from her cheeks and he leaned down. Tenderly, he kissed her softly on her lips. She released a quiet sigh and once again he held her to him. For the first time in an hour, she felt safe.

"Oh Marie, you're safe now." Marie felt his strong arms around him. He was so warm and solid. Marie stretched out, lying back on the bed. Harris curled around her. Again he kissed her sweetly on her cheek. Marie turned to her side and Harris held her, pulling her tightly against him. Through sniffles and kisses, Marie fell into a delicious sleep, wondering if she'd find this wonderful man still holding her in the morning.

The next morning Marie awoke with sunlight creeping across her blanket. She turned over and reached her hand back to feel the empty bed. The door to the room clicked open. Harris pushed it with his elbow, holding a plate covered with flakey pastries in one hand and a small tray with two steaming coffee mugs in his other hand. He stopped for a moment and looked down at her in the bed. Marie pulled the blanket under her chin, discreetly lifting her palm over her mouth and breathing into it to check her breath.

"Good morning, Marie. I thought you might want something for breakfast." Harris moved all the way into the room and placed the food on the corner of the bottom of the bed as Marie sat up. He handed her a mug of café au lait and she sipped it greedily, while leaning back on the headboard. "This morning I put a call in to the American Embassy to my friend Charles. I turned the Milton Fabergé Box over to the authorities there and they'll be returning it to New Orleans overnight in a diplomatic pouch."

Marie looked over at the bedside table, confirming that the little black bag was gone. She sighed with relief. Harris smiled at her and then he pressed his lips together, as if he didn't want to tell her something.

"What is it? What else are you not telling me?" Marie took another sip of the coffee and reached for a croissant. He shifted his gaze from her.

"Uh, you may need to speak with the Embassy about what you know about this Paul guy or Philip Augustus." He picked up a newspaper that was on the other table in the room and handed it to her. She immediately unfolded it and tried to decipher what the headline said in French, but she recognized the large photograph from the front of the George V and a smaller insert photograph of Paul and another man she didn't recognize.

"What does it say?" Marie flipped through the pages of the paper, somehow hoping she'd suddenly understand.

"According to the authorities, this man, Scott Cross or Scott LaCroix," Harris pointed to the picture of the unfamiliar man, "was found murdered in a hotel room at the George V that was registered to Philip Augustus. The authorities suspect that the two men knew each other but are perplexed how an obscure art dealer might know a seedy drug dealer and criminal from Gravesend in London." Marie again attempted to read the words, hoping she'd find out something more, but dropped the paper on her lap and bit into the croissant.

"What do the authorities want with me? I don't really know anything." Marie insisted, tearing off another bite of the pastry and chewing furiously. She thought back to the previous evening.

"Yesterday you said that Paul told you that he didn't steal the Fabergé Box, but he did give it to you yesterday." Harris patted Marie on her knee. "What do you think that means?"

"Well, yesterday I would have thought that he told me the truth. He said that someone else had the box. He even thought that maybe I worked for that LaCroix guy or maybe I worked for the buyer." Marie replayed her conversation with Paul in her head. She tried to remember every detail. "Why would he tell me that if he had the box the whole time?"

"I don't know. Maybe he and LaCroix work together and had a falling out. Maybe he didn't want you to know that he had the box the whole time. Either way, we need to speak with the authorities at the American Embassy. You don't want to end up speaking to them at a French police station, do you?"

Marie's eyes widened at the thought. Was she in serious trouble?

"Donald, am I in trouble?" Marie asked softly, placing her croissant down on the plate. She could feel herself start to sweat.

"No, but I'm not sure that you might not be in danger. You are the only one who can place Paul or Philip Augustus at the George V near the time of the murder," Harris answered matter of fact. He stood up from the bed and stretched his arms out, rotating his neck left and right. Marie gulped.

"Oh no!" Marie exclaimed, pulling the blanket up to her chin. Harris stared down at Marie. He sat down next to her and put his arm around her.

"I'm here. You're going to be just fine. We need to get

going." He pulled her into a hug, kissing her on top of her head. Marie touched the top of her head, attempting to smooth down her hair which had grown wild overnight.

"I better go back to my room and get ready. I'll meet you downstairs in about twenty minutes." Marie scooted off the bed and slipped her feet into her shoes next to the bed. Harris sat on the bed and looked up at her. She looked down at him and smiled. "Wait a minute; you kissed me last night?" Harris offered a coy grin, raising one eyebrow in response.

"I'll see you downstairs in twenty minutes." He took her hand in his and drew it to his lips, pressing a soft kiss on it. Marie shook her head and giggled.

Marie slipped her card into the key reader and pushed open the door to her room. She stepped inside the darkened room, surprised that she hadn't left a lamp on or opened the curtains before she left yesterday. She reached for the nearest table lamp and a hand gripped her wrist. Another hand slapped her across her mouth with such force that her lips and chin stung.

Marie tried to struggle away, but her assailant pulled her tightly toward him. The assailant shook her and hissed: "Don't say a word!" Slowly, the assailant pulled away his hand from her mouth and shoved her backward so she fell on the bed.

Marie immediately scrambled across the bed, pressing herself against the headboard. Someone clicked on a light across the room. Marie scanned her room. Her suitcase was open and clothing strewn across the floor, the mini-fridge door was wide open, and her toiletries case had been dumped on the table near the window.

"Give me your bag!" Marie turned to the demanding voice. She recognized the man as the night manager Jean. She looked at the other man who was slight, with small glasses. Marie held her purse out to Jean and he tore it from her grasp. He threw the bag to the other man who turned the bag upside down and shook out its contents on the floor. "Is anything there, Emile?" Jean asked the other man. Emile shook his head.

Jean stepped closer to the bed and reached for Marie. Marie instinctively scooted from his grasp, falling off the edge of the bed, landing on a pair of heels. Jean rounded the bed and lurched towards her. Marie gripped the shoe, pointing the heel out and swung it at the man's face, making contact with his lower front teeth. He grabbed his lower jaw and stumbled back. Marie took the advantage, grabbing hold of a lamp next to the bed, yanking it towards her. She swung the lamp, making contact with Jean's nose. She immediately turned to the other man and threw the lamp at him, striking him in the face and knocking off his glasses. Marie weaved between the two staggering men to the door, but Jean threw himself against it.

Something inside of Marie snapped. Her fear transformed into rage. Marie screamed so loudly that both men covered their ears. At the same time, she drove the full weight of her body into Jean. He tried to raise his arms, but Marie bit down on his arms, sinking her teeth in until he cried out. Meanwhile, Emile pulled Marie back by the shoulders. She swung her hands back wildly making contact with the man's crouch. He, too, yelped.

Someone pounded on the door. Marie stomped down on Jean's toes and he hopped from blocking the door and she turned and kicked Emile once again between the legs. She pulled open the door and Harris' eyes widened as he looked at Marie and the wreckage behind her.

Harris stepped into the room and closed the door behind him. He looked down at the two groaning men and back at Marie, "What in the world happened in here?" He leaned down and spoke to Jean rapidly in French. The night manager raised his hands in front of his face, insisting something in French. He stepped over to the other man and growled something to him in French. Emile just whimpered.

Marie felt drained and started to shake. She drew in a deep breath: "When I came back to my room, these men were here. They went through my stuff. I don't know what happened. He…" Marie gestured toward Jean, "came for me and I grabbed my shoe and then I swung a lamp and then I threw a lamp and then I got really angry!" Marie started to feel more energized and stepped closer to Jean, something wild in her eyes. Jean's eyes filled with terror. He muttered something about "dangerous American woman."

"Indeed, she is," Harris agreed with Jean's assessment of Marie. She turned her head towards Emile and smiled. Emile turned on his side and moaned. "Marie, stop terrorizing them," Harris smirked as he said it. He pulled Jean to his feet, holding him up and spoke rapidly in French, shaking him when he didn't respond immediately.

"What is he saying? Why did they dump out my stuff? What were they doing in my room?" Marie tried to look over Harris' shoulder as he spoke to Jean. Harris looked over his shoulder at Marie.

"Marie, would you give me a second? I'll tell you what he said in a minute. I tell you what, watch that other guy, okay? I might need to speak to him in a minute." Marie nodded. She picked up the mangled lamp and sat down on the bed and leaned over Emile.

"What were you doing in my room?" Marie leaned over Emile and whispered quietly. Emile shook his head and pressed his lips closed. "You should go ahead a tell me. You know what, I'm not feeling all that well." She dropped the lamp on the man and tried to cover her mouth.

"Non!" Emile shouted as Marie sneezed straight into the

man's face. He grimaced in disgust.

"You should talk to me. I have allergies and that'll probably happen again," Marie said earnestly. She wiggled her nose as if preparing to sneeze again. Emile nodded.

"Please, don't do that again. I'm sorry. We knew that Philip gave you something. He called me last night. He told us to get it from your room and take it to him, but we couldn't find it." Emile shrugged his shoulders.

"He told you to attack me in my room?" Marie demanded from the man. Emile shrugged. "Tell me, did he say to hurt me and scare me?"

"We were supposed to get it. We waited until morning. We thought you left the room, but then you returned. I'm sorry."

"Did you follow me from the George V?" Marie asked Emile. He shook his head "no" and offered a blank stare. Marie thought about Emile's words for a moment. She listened to Harris growling out questions in French. Jean was mumbling answers. He sounded like he was almost crying.

Emile slowly sat up, raising his hands above his head in surrender. "Will you call the police?" Emile asked, chewing on his lower lip. He listened intently to Harris and Jean.

Marie ignored his question, leaned closer to Emile, "Who is LaCroix?" Emile's eyes widened. Emile shook his head, refusing to speak.

Marie feigned that she was about to sneeze, "I think I'm allergic to something in this room and I can't find a tissue because of this mess." Marie pressed a finger under her nose, as if holding off the sneeze.

"Non, please!" Emile's face twisted in disgust. "Okay, I will talk. LaCroix is just a criminal. He's not even French."

"Why would Paul kill him? Was it for the Fabergé box?" Marie pressed on.

"Non, c'est impossible! Paul would never do that," Emile insisted, "He's a thief, but he would never kill anyone."

"Does—I mean, did—Paul know LaCroix?" Marie continued.

Emile shrugged his shoulders, "They grew up together. They were—what is the word for *voisin*?" Marie wrinkled her brow, wondering. "They live on the same street?" Emile suggested. Marie nodded in understanding.

Harris finished his conversation with Jean and dropped the man to the floor. The two men sat for a moment and then looked up at Harris. He crossed his arms and pressed his lips together, making his Clint Eastwood expression.

"You said, if I answered your questions, we could go." Jean spoke from the floor. He looked between Marie and Harris. Harris stepped to the door and pulled it open. The two men scrambled to their feet to flee, stumbling through the doorway and into the hallway.

Harris slammed shut the door behind the two fools. He walked over to Marie and pulled her into an embrace. He kissed her and Marie felt butterflies. She leaned back in the embrace to search the expression on his face. His gruff expression melted into a mellow smile. Marie could not help but laugh.

"Are you okay, Marie?" Harris asked sweetly, gently kissing her cheek. Marie nodded.

"Yes, but I was scared for a little bit, and then I felt mad, now I'm just tired. What did Jean tell you?" Marie asked. She laced her fingers behind Harris' neck.

"Paul called them and told them that you had the box. He wanted them to retrieve it quietly. They waited until early this morning, when they thought you'd leave your room, and then they would take it, but they realized that you didn't head back to your room last night so they waited." Marie nodded and let out a long breath.

"Why did you let them go?" Marie looked toward the door, wondering if the two would return.

"I frightened them—or rather I think that you frightened them—enough. I got what I needed to know about this thief's operation here, and Jean knows that I can find him if I want to. That really frightened him. By the way, you're getting comped for your entire stay here at Hotel Marguerite." Marie scanned the messy room.

"Why don't I straighten this up while you get ready for our appointment at the American Embassy? I'll wait for you right out here." Harris reluctantly released Marie from his arms and bent down and picked up a mangled lamp. Marie smiled and entered the bathroom.

Chapter 16

Paul leaned against the wall between two rubbish bins in a wet alleyway. He kicked the bin on his right after he hung up with Emile. The Fabergé Box was gone. The paintings were gone. The police were poking around.

Paul pushed the image of LaCroix's hotel room from his mind, but strangely he could still smell that sickening copper odor. He looked down at his watch. The rendezvous was set for now, but he was hiding in an alleyway, empty-handed across from the red-awninged Napoleon Café on Rue d'Estrées, only a few blocks from the Hotel des Invalides. Should he enter the café?

Paul almost emerged from his shadowy spot except something about the man sitting at the small table in front of the café caught his eye. The man appeared to be engrossed, reading his newspaper and sipping a small cup of coffee, but every now and then, he would touch his ear and seem to cough into his fist. He looked at the other diners, recognizing the telltale signs of undercover police.

Silently, he moved deeper into the alleyway, emerging on the next street. He weaved through the crowded sidewalks for two blocks until he found another alleyway and entered it. He pulled out his phone a dialed the familiar number, listening to the rings.

"Hello, Mr. Smith," the cold mechanical voice answered. Hearing the voice say his real name shocked him. "Did you find the box with LaCroix? Are you on your way to the Napoleon Café near the Hotel des Invalides?" the voice cackled. Paul held the phone from his ear. "I thought you'd appreciate meeting near the final burial place of another man who pretended to be a king."

Paul felt a chill run down his body. Whoever the voice was knew who he was. He or she knew his name. He or she knew his cover.

"Did you kill LaCroix?" Paul whispered into the phone, holding his breath, waiting for the answer. The line fell silent. "Did you?" Paul prompted.

"No, Philip Augustus killed LaCroix; isn't that right?" The voice laughed and Paul clenched his teeth. "Losing someone you love, losing an old friend is painful, isn't it? At least he died fairly quickly. Some are not that blessed. Some die slowly over twenty years and that is heartbreaking to endure, trying to help and knowing that you are powerless to prevent the poison they willingly ingested," the voice answered. Then it sighed, "Well, Mr. Smith, do you have the box or not?"

Paul ground his teeth, pressing his eyes closed, "No, I don't have it."

"Do you know where it is now? Because I do." The voice spoke with a sing-songy tone and laughed.

"Where is it?" Paul leaned back on the wall. He didn't know why he asked. Why was he still speaking with this unknown person?

"Why, sir, it is headed back to New Orleans in a diplomatic bag as we speak. It seems someone delivered it to the American Embassy this morning. Perhaps you could go and pick it up in New Orleans. The weather is lovely there, I hear," the voice chirped cheerfully.

"Why would I do that? I'm done. You killed LaCroix. Who are you?" Paul shouted into the phone. He balled his hands into fists, trying to contain his anger.

"What do you care about the why or the who? You have another opportunity to steal that box. What do you care? You are a thief and a criminal, dragging innocent people into your life. Do you want another chance?" the voice taunted Paul. "$750,000. I will give you ten minutes to think about it and call me back."

The phone clicked off. Paul held the phone to his chest, trying to slow his breathing. He needed to focus, to remember what the voice had said. What did it mean about dragging innocent people into his life? Paul shook his head, clearing his thoughts. This person seemed to know him. He should just walk away now, but how could he? The store was closed, his cover blown, and his face was probably on an Interpol watch list. He needed money to do anything. He also needed to know why.

He hit the redial button and the voice immediately answered, "I thought you would call back, Mr. Smith. When can I expect to see you in New Orleans?" Paul's heart sank.

Marie and Harris spent two hours at the American Embassy. Marie felt a little tired, but she also felt excited. The two strolled over to the Champs Elysées and headed toward the Place de la Concorde. One side of the famous boulevard was lined with Ferraris. Tourists surrounded the cars and snapped pictures with their phones. Marie and Harris laughed at the spectacle of it all.

They made it to the Place de la Concorde and then to the Jardin des Tuileries. In the shade of a tree, across from a playground, the two sat. They were silent for a moment, watching children play. Marie took Harris' hand and laced her fingers between his.

"I think that we should go to dinner tonight," Harris suggested. He cocked his head to the side and looked at her. His grey eyes filled with hope at her response. Marie nodded enthusiastically.

That evening, Marie and Harris met in the lobby of the Hotel Maguerite. They looked at each other. Marie twirled around and her black skirt swirled. The two laughed and linked arms, heading to the restaurant down the street from the hotel.

The bistro was filled with small tables covered in starched white tablecloths and flickering tea lights. Soft candlelight bathed the restaurant. The lighting drew out the red and gold hues in the decor. Harris gently helped Marie into her seat. The waiter spoke to them briefly, handed them their menus, and scurried away. Another couple sat across the restaurant from them, leaning their heads so close together that they almost touched over the middle of their table.

In the corner of the room, a small trio arranged their instruments and began softly playing. Marie was dazzled, "This must be the most romantic restaurant in the whole of Paris." Harris nodded in agreement and started to read his menu. Marie tried to decipher what the dishes were and Harris explained what each item was patiently.

The waiter poured them their wine. Harris swirled the wine in his glass, inspecting it before trying it and nodding approvingly. Marie sipped the wine and put down her glass,

"Do you really think that Paul killed that man for the Fabergé Box?"

Harris wrinkled his nose as if smelling something unpleasant and took a sip, "Does it really matter?"

"Yes, it matters. A man was murdered. Do you really think that Paul could have done it?" Marie rested her chin on her fists and waited for Harris' response. He put down his glass and his gaze rose to the ceiling, considering her question.

"It certainly seems that way. It appears that they might have known each other or known of each other. They are both criminals. Paul had blood on him when he gave you the box. I'm sure there are more details that will come out." Harris lifted his glass and swirled the liquid around. "Of course it could have been someone else, but that's unlikely." He took another sip.

Marie considered what he said and remembered looking into Paul's blue eyes. He had looked distressed and pained. He didn't seem like a murderer, but what did she actually know about the man? Marie's thoughts were interrupted when the waiter delivered the first course of their dinner.

The meal tasted wonderful. Marie and Harris enjoyed three courses and two bottles of red wine over a leisurely three hours. They laughed and talked about their lives. He spoke about investigating art thefts and the excitement at recovering the stolen items. Marie felt in awe of his experiences. As Marie bit down on the glorious chocolate confection she had for dessert, Harris sipped his coffee and spoke: "Marie, you really are quite smart and funny, so I know you're probably really good at what you do for a living…" Marie snorted and the two laughed, "But why do you work at that job? I think you could be doing so much more. It sounds boring."

Marie put down her fork and thought, "You know, Harris, it is boring. I took the job a few years ago after working several years as an assistant librarian. My ex-husband suggested that I needed a new job that paid better. I thought I was going to participate in lots of community work at the non-profit, but instead I spend my day researching grants, donors and similar organizations; checking reports for errors, editing publications." Marie rattled off her duties. *Wow, it really was boring*, she thought.

"What would you like to do?" Harris asked, as he lowered his cup from his lips, listening for her answer.

"I don't know. I guess that's part of the reason for this trip. I'm trying new things," Marie answered honestly. "But I think that I'd like to do something like what you're doing. Solving mysteries…"

"And rescuing artwork?" Harris and Marie laughed. Harris cleared his throat, "You have skills, Marie. I think that you could do what I do."

Marie bit down on her cake, tucking the idea away. "Do you have a girlfriend back home?" She couldn't believe that she'd asked such a bold question but the words blurted out. Harris' expression went blank as he sipped his coffee.

"I would certainly hope not after this evening," he answered. Marie giggled. Harris stared into her eyes. She drew a shallow breath and put down her fork. Harris signaled the waiter for the check.

The next morning, Harris and Marie returned to the Tuileries and wandered around. At one end of the Gardens, they found a flower cart and Harris bought Marie a small bouquet. She pressed her nose into the flowers and breathed in the scent. They found their bench from the previous day and sat. She took his hand and again breathed in the flowers with a delighted sigh.

"You know, despite the scary stuff, I'm really having a lot of fun." Marie smiled radiantly at Harris. She wanted to say more, but she figured blurting out, "I think you're amazing," might frighten him away. She liked learning more about this accomplished man. She liked the way he kissed her. She wondered if he wanted to marry her. Maybe she was getting a little ahead of herself? She just needed to be cool. "I think you're super sexy!" Yes, cool had definitely flown out the window.

Marie sunk into the bench as Harris rocked with laughter, "I like you a lot too, Marie." Marie blushed bright red as the two shook with laughter. "But it might just be the Paris effect."

Marie stopped laughing and examined Harris closely. His gaze fixed on some unknown object in the park. He then looked at her seriously. Marie opened her mouth to speak and then shut it. She suddenly felt like a deflated balloon, pulling her hand from his.

"Is that what you really think? Am I just intoxicated by the romance of Paris and travel that I wouldn't know whether or not I liked someone or found them attractive?" Harris wrinkled his brow with concern, trying to think how to answer Marie.

"No, that isn't what I'm trying to say. I'm saying that this is fun, but in a few days you'll head back to New Orleans. I'll be making my report to the New Orleans Museum's board. Then we will go back to our regular lives." Harris realized as soon as he spoke how much he'd hurt Marie. She breathed slowly, trying not to cry. She bit her lip.

"Maybe the whole reason why I came to Paris was not to follow some thief or find some stolen artwork or kiss you, but just to return to New Orleans as boring old Marie. Maybe this could be the start of an incredible relationship, Harris. Maybe this is the start of me really living." Marie stood up at the bench and glanced down at Harris. He opened and closed his mouth, not sure what to say. "Maybe it is the Paris effect or maybe you're just afraid. I've been afraid for a long time, but I'm not afraid of this, but I think that you are." She held Harris' cheek in her hand. He closed his eyes.

She put down her flowers and reached into her purse and pulled out her map, opening it and flipping it over. "You know what? I'm not afraid. If you'll excuse me, this is my vacation and I have a lot more of Paris to see before I leave in three days."

Marie walked away before Harris could even respond. Her eyes caught a glimpse of a sign for the Louvre. She nodded to herself. She was going live her trip and while she was at it, she would stop for an ice cream cone on the other end of the park.

Chapter 17

Marie spent the next few days checking items off her bucket list. She drank hot chocolate at Angelina on Rue de Rivoli. She bought macarons at Ladurée and then rode the huge Ferris wheel at the Place de la Concorde at night. She crossed the Pont Alexandre III and the Pont Neuf.

On her second to last day in the afternoon, she remembered her conversation with Ms. Green on the flight to Atlanta. She asked the woman behind the desk at her hotel about the fake building in the 10th arrondissement. The woman tapped her finger on her lips and started tapping on the computer. She grabbed a map, pulled out a highlighter and marked a path for Marie to follow to 145 Rue de la Fayette. Marie thanked her and set off on her way.

Marie set off to see the fake building. She traveled leisurely down Rue de Sevres, and then crossed the Pont du Carousel. She stopped in the middle of the bridge and checked the map, realizing it might have been easier to have taken the Metro. She skirted the Louvre and headed down Rue de Richelieu and eventually found Rue de La Fayette. She read each street number as she drew closer.

Finally, she stood before the building and looked up. She wasn't sure it was right so she moved closer. Surely it wasn't this building? Was it? Marie stepped closer and noticed there were no doorknobs or handles. A small detail gave away the building's fraud.

She leaned closer to the building. Tourists walked passed her. One stared puzzled at her leaning her head near the building. She wondered if she could hear the Metro or sounds from its exhaust. The façade hid its secret well. Marie took a picture with her phone. She would need to tell Lauren about the spot. Then, she returned to her hotel.

Walking back, her thoughts drifted to Harris. She would have liked to have shared the discovery of this piece of Paris with him. She wanted to talk with him, but she pushed the thought away. He was now avoiding her and it didn't seem like she would get a chance to see him before she left Paris the day after tomorrow. Perhaps Harris was correct and her feelings were just a Paris effect, but the lump in her throat suggested otherwise.

In the days following the episode with Jean, the night manager, Marie noticed that the staff of the Hotel Maguerite lavished attention on her. She found chocolates in her room and extra towels. When she went downstairs, they offered her glasses of wine and snacks, while complimenting her profusely. She even received a voucher for a boat tour on the Seine which she took on her last day. Floating along the Seine, she finally saw Notre Dame which she could not get close enough to see earlier in the week because of the repairs after the fire of 2019.

On her last night, she headed to the Bon Marche and found a bottle of champagne and some snacks. After making her purchases, she returned to the hotel. As usual, the person at the front desk rushed around the counter to help her carry her purchases. Marie smiled and shooed her away. She approached the desk and the clerk immediately offered her a candy which Marie happily took, "I was wondering if I might have a glass and maybe a basket to take my wine and food to the park at the Eiffel Tower."

The clerk's eyes filled with delight. The young woman pressed her hands together in a prayer pose and shook her head. "Of course, Madame. I will be right back. Please stay right here." The girl rushed around the desk and headed to the other side of the lobby through the door to the kitchen. She returned with a cute basket and gestured for Marie to hand her the bottle of champagne and snacks. The woman took the items, turned with a flourish and packed the basket. With the same flourish she turned back around and handed the basket to Marie.

Marie thanked the woman and exited the hotel, making her way for the last time on her trip to the Eiffel Tower. She smiled to herself thinking about all that she had experienced in the last two days. She wondered what had happened to Paul, the thief. Could it only have been four days before that she'd carried the Milton Fabergé Box in her purse? Did Paul really kill LaCroix? Sadness tugged at her as she wondered if Harris was thinking about her at all.

She made it to the Parc du Champ de Mars in record time. Other tourists seemed to have the same idea as Marie. She tried to find an empty bench or space on the green. Finally, she found a spot near a small tree and pulled off her cardigan to place on the ground.

"I brought a blanket."

Marie turned to the familiar voice. Harris held a green and blue plaid blanket. Marie put down the basket and took two corners of the blanket, stretching it out on the ground.

"What are you doing here?" Marie asked as she settled into her spot, pulling the basket close to open it.

"I've been missing you the last couple of days..." Harris' voice trailed off. Marie waited for him to continue his sentence. She reached into the basket and pulled out the champagne. She examined the label and realized it was not the bottle she'd purchased but a Dom Perignon.

"What the heck?" Marie exclaimed. Harris' face fell, but Marie quickly reassured him, "No, not you; it's the champagne." Harris sat down on the blanket, crossing his legs like a little child. "So, you missed me?"

"Yes, I did; I do," Harris spoke deliberately. He eyed the bottle, "You want me to open that for you?" Marie was about to protest that she only had one glass but upon further inspection of the basket she discovered two champagne flutes, and a huge assortment of French cheeses and patés with bread in addition to the few snacks she'd bought.

"Yes, you open the bottle; I'll pull out the snacks." At that moment, the tower began to sparkle in the dark with a light show. Marie marveled at the beauty. She would miss Paris when she left tomorrow.

Thoughts about home crept in: How would work be when she returned? Would she just go back to her rut? Would Harris be there too? She pushed the thoughts away. She would enjoy this time right now. Right now she didn't care if it was the Paris Effect, she was exactly where she wanted to be.

Chapter 18

Marie was bleary-eyed and exhausted when she put her key into the lock of her front door. She turned the knob and pulled her suitcase behind her, huffing and puffing into her living room. Her phone chirped and she answered it.

"Hello, Marie; it's me. Are you home yet?" Lauren sang into the phone. Marie smiled at her sister's voice.

"I'm just getting in, Lauren. How are you? Everyone feeling better after the flu?" Marie shut the door behind her and leaned against it, dropping her key in the basket on the table next to her front door. She glanced into the mirror. She examined her reflection critically: her brown hair fell flat to her shoulders, her eyes appeared puffy and her lips were chapped. She stuck out her tongue.

"Well, now, I'm getting over the flu, but things are good. Robbie and I spoke more than we have in weeks. Lance is going to take this week off. Tell me, how was your trip?" Marie could imagine Lauren smiling, comfortably sitting under her white comforter. Marie heard something rustle behind her. She clicked on the overhead light.

"Welcome home from Paris!" Paul stood in her living room. Paul the Thief was standing in her living room greeting her. Marie opened her mouth to scream, but he put his index finger over his lips.

"Uh, Lauren, the trip was eventful. I better go. Bye." Marie clicked off her phone, putting it back in her purse. She stepped into the living room.

"What are you doing here? Inside my house? How do you even know where I live?" Marie asked incredulously. She paced the room and collapsed onto the couch. Realizing she'd just put the phone back in her purse, she began to rummage through it for her phone.

"Please, don't do that." Paul sat down next to Marie and she immediately stood up and moved to the overstuffed chair. Marie held her phone and carefully placed it on the arm of the chair.

"Let me repeat my questions: What are you doing here, inside my house? And how do you know where I live?" Marie crossed her arms across her chest. Paul lifted both palms up in a show of innocence.

"I need your help. I don't have anywhere else to go right now in New Orleans and you're probably the only person I know who lives here. You know, you figured out where I lived, so why shouldn't I be able to figure out where you live?" Paul tossed the question back at Marie adding, "I looked you up on the Internet white pages."

Marie rolled her eyes until she thought about LaCroix. Had Paul killed LaCroix? Was a killer sitting on her couch in her living room? Why was he in New Orleans? "Did you kill that man LaCroix?"

Paul pressed his lips together, "No, I did not kill him. I overheard who shot him, but I didn't see them. I got there when he was dying."

"Okay," she said slowly, "I think I believe you, but why are you in New Orleans? Seems pretty far from Paris and that maybe since you stole artwork from the museum here you might not be in the smartest place for you?" Marie suggested to Paul. He smiled sheepishly and stretched his legs in front of him and his arms across the back of the couch. He didn't appear to want to answer the question, so she pressed on: "How did you know LaCroix?" Paul shifted his gaze from Marie to one of her bookshelves, again ignoring her question. Marie drew in a breath, "Emile said you grew up on the same street as LaCroix, you knew each other as children. Did you work together to steal the artwork?"

Paul straightened in his seat and leaned forward. "You talked to Emile?" Paul's expression was perplexed. Marie crossed her arms and examined Paul's expression.

"I met him when he and that night manager attacked me in my room trying to find the Milton Fabergé Box," Marie answered pointedly. Paul raised his eyebrows in surprise.

"I didn't mean for that to happen. I just thought I could get it back," Paul answered slowly. Marie nodded her head, realizing that he'd just used her to transport stolen goods while a man died.

"I think you should leave right now." Marie stood up and pointed at the front door. Paul pressed his palms together and released a sigh.

"Marie, please, I need your help!" Paul pleaded, his blue eyes appearing to water.

"My help for what? My help to give you a place to stay so you can do something illegal? I need answers and you think that you can bat your eyelashes, waltz in here, and I will foolishly say 'okay' because you're handsome and I'm desperate?" Marie was almost growling at this point.

"Okay, I'll answer your questions, but please let me stay." Paul now stood toe to toe with Marie. Marie stepped back, her calves brushing against the chair.

"Step back and sit down!" Marie commanded. Paul nodded and returned to his spot on the couch. "Okay, why are you here? Are you planning on stealing something and why?"

Two hours later, Marie stumbled into her bedroom and collapsed onto her bed, shutting the bedroom door behind her. She felt exhausted. She'd left Paul arranging sheets on the couch, preparing to sleep. Crawling under the crisp cool sheets, she tossed from side to side. Was she doing the right thing?

Despite all her questions, Marie still felt unsure and unsettled about her overnight guest. Was he telling her the truth? Was he really going to steal the Milton Fabergé Box to discover who might have killed LaCroix? He was still evasive about their relationship, as if embarrassed about speaking about his youth. Or was this just another opportunity for him to grab the box and collect a big payday?

She turned over and pounded her pillow thinking about her last questions for the evening. Paul was stretched out on the couch and muttering to himself. Marie wanted to know, so she stormed into her living room and asked: "Why did you use the name of Prince Philip and that other king's name? Do you always choose a 'King Philip'?" Marie leaned forward awaiting his answer.

Paul rolled his head toward her and smiled, "You noticed that? I guess I like to play pretend that I'm someone completely different—the total opposite of how I grew up." Marie found the answer sweet, but realized that he was trying to distract her with his charm.

"I am sure that's partly true, but I'm also sure there's more to it." Marie pressed. Paul turned over on the couch. She could not see his face and could barely hear his response.

"As it is for all our childhoods. We are either running away from it or toward it when we start to feel some regret, I suppose." Marie wished to press further, but she could hear a soft snore.

Marie thought about the exchange and shook her head and went back to her bed. Either way, after tomorrow morning, he would leave and Marie would return to work. She would probably never see him again and life would return to normal. *Yes, normal,* Marie thought grimly. Marie's eyelids felt like lead and shut.

The alarm chirped in Marie's ear. She didn't feel like she'd had eight hours of sleep. She felt like she'd just closed and opened her eyes. Marie staggered into the kitchen to start the coffee maker and released a howl upon seeing a half-naked man lying on her couch until she remembered what had happened last night. She quietly tiptoed to her bathroom, while the coffee dripped. She took her shower, dressed and returned to the kitchen to find Paul, fully clothed, leaning on her kitchen counter, sipping a mug of steaming coffee. She noticed he didn't pour her a mug.

"Great, you're up. I need to go into work. They have asked the 'inessential workers' to come in, and remove our personal items. We're all getting new computers and there is some new rodent protocol to review before I can return in another week. You can let yourself out." Marie poured herself a mug and moved to the door. Paul just watched her leave.

Marie tried to put the image of Paul leaning on her kitchen counter out of her mind. She hopped into her car and headed to the office. Block by block she rode, wondering about what Paul had told her. He was going after the Milton Fabergé Box again.

What should she do? Should she tell Harris, the police? Would she get in trouble? Wait—she would definitely get in trouble. The man was staying at her house, sipping her coffee, probably showering in her shower as she drove. With that image in her head, she almost hit a parked car and forced herself to refocus. She needed to go to work.

The office this morning was mostly empty. It smelled like fresh paint and plastic. Marie approached her cubicle which looked troublingly sterile, a cardboard box on her desk was filled with waterlogged personal items. A few folks milled around the offices, avoiding eye contact and talking. This was not a good sign.

Slowly, she approached the conference room. David, her boss, stood at one end of the table. Lisa and Tina sat next to each other, near him, copiously scribbling in yellow pads and nodding. Marie attempted to subtly pivot and hide, but she heard David call her name.

"Marie, may I have a word with you here in the conference room? Thank you so much for coming in today. I know it was hard." Marie turned to the sound of David's voice. Her shoulders immediately tightened as she slowly walked to the conference room.

When she entered the room, she noticed that Tina and Lisa didn't move. Marie had the distinct feeling that David was about to fire her, but she wondered if he would really do it in front of those two? She knew they thought she was boring, but were they really that cruel?

Marie entered the conference room and took a seat in a swivel chair, opposite Tina and Lisa. The two smiled at her like Cheshire cats. Marie knew immediately that this was not a friendly chat. David remained standing at the end of the table.

"Marie, I believe that you have been with this organization for what—two years?" David asked with an ingratiating grin. He was trying to sound sincere, but the effect was smarmy.

"Actually, I've worked here for three years as an assistant to the editor of publications and research. Any internal or external report I check for errors. I help write the content for the publications that we send to donors. I call donors and receive calls from them. I also assist as a liaison between other organizations that do similar work to us and help coordinate our efforts." Marie immediately rattled off her job description. She watched as Tina scribbled down her every word. She pressed her lips together and waited for Tina to look up.

"I see," David again smiled more broadly now. "It sounds like a lot." David nodded his head and Tina and Lisa nodded their heads like bobble head dolls. Marie looked at David and then swiveled her chair to look at Tina and Lisa. The room became very quiet.

"I guess it can be sometimes, but I enjoy what I do," Marie answered. The three glanced back and forth at each other. What were they planning? They were definitely up to something, but what? Marie tried to relax and pay attention.

"I am sure that you are aware that Tina and Lisa are skilled at marketing. I have a special project for them..." David began.

"Really, what is it?" Marie interrupted. David smiled tightly. Marie could see a vein in his neck bulge.

"It's a major project..." David sputtered. "So they will need your help." David nodded as if convincing himself of what he was saying. Again, Lisa and Tina nodded like bobble head dolls.

"Wow, that's great. I'd love to work on this project with you two. Tell me all about it and how I can help," Marie offered brightly. She pulled her notebook from her bag and clicked her pen at the ready to write. Tina and Lisa looked at each other in horror. Marie could feel red creep up her neck.

"Uh, well, it isn't really like that, Marie. What they need is for you to show them what you've been doing, give them your connections in the community, maybe turn over your notes to them about how you do your job here?" David gestured with his hands like he was conducting a symphony—a symphony of her job's demise.

Marie stared at David. David stared at Marie, waiting for her to speak. His smile slowly dropped. He placed both his palms on the table. Lisa and Tina scooted back in their chairs. Marie mirrored his posture and placed both her hands on the table. She needed to think. She needed to get out of there.

As if on cue, an administrative assistant knocked on the conference room door and peeked in. "Sorry to interrupt, but Marie, you have an urgent phone call from a Philip La-belle, or maybe le-belle?" Marie's jaw dropped and she immediately stood up.

"Clare, you should just take a message. We're right in the middle of something here. I'm sure that Tina or Lisa can call this gentleman right back when we're finished..." David hinted at what he was doing to the assistant and the woman turned red.

"But, it's an international call. He said that he must speak with Marie and would only speak with Marie about his donation. They know each other from Paris. He said she was the only one who could understand. He needed someone..." she hesitated before she spoke, "..he said that knew more than, I quote: 'those two bubble heads.' He did not specify who he meant by 'bubble heads.'" The assistant shrank back from the doorway. Lisa and Tina looked perplexed. David looked furious.

"I guess I'd better go take care of that and we can get back to this in just a few moments. I'm sure Monsieur le Bel meant two other 'bubble heads.'" Marie pivoted and ran through the doorway to her desk. At her desk, she picked up her phone, turning to see David, Tina and Lisa arguing in the conference room as they all glared at Marie.

"Your highness, how may I help you? You really went with Philip the Fair? Are you kidding me?" Marie asked. Paul laughed on the other end of the phone. She could hear he was rustling around with something.

"Marie, Marie, so glad you picked up. I called your cell, but you must not have had it on you or turned it off so I called your office. That assistant sounded very hesitant about letting me speak with you, so I had to do something. Everything okay at your rodent infestation protocol seminar?" Paul asked innocently. She couldn't help but smile. She released a sigh and glanced back at the conference room. The three continued to argue, but now David was gesturing toward her.

"I think that I'm in the middle of being canned in the presence of two bubble heads so your call could not have come at a better time. Is everything okay? Are you still at my apartment?" Marie asked. David, Tina and Lisa stood up. "Quick, they're coming this way. What's up?"

"Wait, they're going to fire you? That's terrible. Should I speak with them?" Paul teased. "Okay, three things, some courier dropped off a really official envelope for you; want me to open it and read it to you?"

"No, is that it? They're coming over here. I need to figure something out now and get off the phone," Marie insisted. She turned her back on the conference room, but she could see them gathering their items.

"Two other things: Would you give me a lift to the museum? I need to see where the Milton Fabergé Box is now and…" Paul rattled on. David and the bobble head twins marched toward

Marie's desk.

"No, I'm not going to help you steal that box," Marie hissed in a whisper. Paul chuckled again.

"It would get you out of the office. Also, you have run out of shampoo. I thought I'd go pick up another bottle. What is your preference?"

Marie gritted her teeth. "You're supposed to have left my apartment by now. Please don't go pick up any shampoo, just leave…" Marie stretched out the last part of her sentence. David and company stood directly behind Marie and must have heard the last exchange.

"Uh, yes, Monsieur le Bel, I'll put all those figures together for you. I'll work on this right now. I should hang up." Marie smiled as she spoke. David glared down at Marie and offered his hand. "It seems that my boss would like to speak with you, Monsieur." Marie handed him the receiver.

Before David could speak, Marie could hear a screed of French coming from the receiver. David's face paled and he stuttered, "I'm sorry. I don't understand. Would you say that in English?"

Whatever Paul said next made David pull at his collar uncomfortably. "…oh that's a tremendous amount of money… no I had no idea she did that for you…yes, sir. I mean, oui, sir, monsieur." David laughed nervously. He clumsily replaced the phone in its cradle.

"David, don't we really need to get back to our 'project' that Marie is supposed to help with? Wasn't she supposed to help us with it today only and not come back?" Tina offered in a whiney voice. She tapped her pen against her yellow pad.

David straightened his tie and breathed in, "Uh, no, we can talk about this project when Marie is back from furlough. She will be helping us secure a very large donation. Marie, I believe that you need to help Mr. LaBelle?" David swallowed hard, somewhat staggering from Marie's desk. Tina and Lisa chased behind David, practically stepping on the heels of his shoes.

Marie smiled as David and his toadies scampered away. She wondered what Paul had said, but whatever it was, it had worked for the moment. She sank into her desk chair a moment longer, wondering if she should pick up Paul. Certainly, wasn't it against the law to aid a thief in stealing? On the other hand, she needed to get out of the office before David's nerve returned.

Her cellphone rang in her purse and she answered without even looking at the display. She recognized the voice immediately as he cleared his throat. "Hello, Marie. It's Donald. Uh, do you have a moment to speak?"

"Yes!" She chirped out and then took a breath. What would she tell Harris about Paul being in her apartment? Right now the man was taking a shower, using her soap, planning a heist.

"Oh good, I was wondering if you'd like to grab lunch today. I have some really great news for you. Have you received something today?" Harris asked expectantly.

Before Marie could stop herself she answered: "Paul said that something was dropped off at the apartment this morning and I told him not to open it." Marie wished she could pull back the words she'd just spoken.

"Paul is at your apartment! Marie, what is going on?" Harris demanded. Marie held the phone from her ear. She could hear him shouting to someone else, but she couldn't make out what he was telling that person. She assumed it would mean a SWAT team knocking down her front door and then a few additional police officers also dragging her away.

"Yes, when I returned last night, he was in my apartment," Marie began to explain as she stood up, collecting her box of belongings. "I told him he should leave," Marie offered weakly.

"Yes, but he was there this morning and speaking with you. The man is a murderer," Harris growled the words out through what Marie could only assume were gritted teeth. She had to give it to Harris. He didn't miss a beat.

"He is an alleged murderer. That is true, but I questioned him last night and I don't think that he killed LaCroix. They knew each other growing up..." Marie tried to explain.

She started walking to the front of the building. She could see Tina and Lisa scurrying to their desks. She overheard Tina ask Lisa: "How do you spell LaBelle? How am I supposed to look this guy up?" Marie rolled her eyes.

At last she stood at the front door of the building. Harris was continuing with his lecture when Marie interrupted: "Where do you want to meet?"

Chapter 19

Marie and Harris agreed to meet at her apartment. He arrived at the same time she did. As she walked to her front door, Harris signaled her to be quiet. Marie slipped the key in the lock and turned it. Immediately, Harris rushed through the open door. Marie followed Harris.

Looking around the apartment, Harris slumped. Marie peeked around him, noticing that it appeared that Paul had tidied up the apartment before he left, leaving no trace, except in the bathroom. Marie noticed a slight odor of peroxide. At least the living room was clean. Harris next marched into Marie's bedroom; his eye fell to her made bed. An official looking envelope was perched on her pillow.

Marie wandered to her bed and picked up the envelope and opened it. "Wait, before you open that. I wanted to talk to you about it before I found out the 'Kissy Thief' was hiding out at your house." Harris pulled out his phone and began to dial quickly. He left the room. Marie followed him to the living room and sat down on the couch. She turned the envelope over and over in her hands, wondering about the content.

Harris finished his conversation and sat down across from Marie on the overstuffed chair. He pulled off his glasses and cleaned them. He pressed his index finger to his forehead, "Please tell me again what Paul the Thief was doing here last night." He looked away from Marie and muttered to himself, "please let it not have been kissing."

Marie could not help but laugh at Harris. He turned to her and frowned for a moment. She shook her head *no* and for the first time since he'd entered the apartment, Harris relaxed and his expression softened. "Please tell me everything that you can think of about what he said and what he said he might be doing here in New Orleans."

"Would you like a cup of coffee?" Marie offered sweetly. Harris smiled broadly and nodded. Marie entered the kitchen and started the coffee pot. "Okay, it was like I said earlier. When I got home, he was already in my apartment. I was pretty shocked and told him he needed to leave, but he said he had nowhere to go. At first, he wouldn't tell me what he was doing here, but eventually he told me that he is going after the Milton Fabergé Box again."

Harris moved to the kitchen and started opening cabinets, looking for mugs. He found the correct cabinet and pulled out two. Marie reached for the coffee pot, but Harris tapped her softly on the arm, "Please, let me do this for you." He poured them both cups of coffee. Marie pulled out the milk and grabbed the sugar bowl and presented them to Harris. As they prepared their coffee, he asked: "Did he say why he was going after the box again? That seems really reckless."

Harris puzzled this idea in his head. The two returned to the living room and sat. Harris put down his cup and pulled out his notebook. He flipped through the pages of it, found a new page, and pulled out his pen.

"I thought the same thing," said Marie. "He thinks that the buyer is involved with LaCroix's death. He thinks that maybe if he can identify them then he might be able to clear his name." Marie agreed with Harris, sipping her coffee. Harris wrinkled his brow, then looked up and examined Marie's couch.

"Did he sleep on that couch?" Harris asked, squinting his eyes and curling his lip in disgust. He was attempting his harsh Clint Eastwood look but instead he reminded Marie of a snarling teenager. "Let's switch seats. I can't concentrate right here." The two switched places. "That's better. I find it interesting or suspicious that this buyer still wants this particular piece. I wonder why." Harris tapped his pen on his small notebook. "What else did you learn about this guy?"

"Well, I don't think that he killed LaCroix. He might be a thief and self-involved..." Harris snorted at Marie's description of Paul, "but he doesn't seem like a murderer. He didn't want to say anything about it, but remember what Emile told me at the hotel—he grew up with LaCroix, they lived on the same street. Didn't seem like he liked LaCroix though..." Marie thought back to the previous evening, reflecting on what Paul had said. She wished she had a notebook like Harris.

"Just because they grew up together doesn't mean he didn't kill the man. Most murders are between people who know each other." Harris spoke matter-of-factly. Marie pondered Harris' words. She sucked in a breath; something was nagging at her.

"'Most murders are between people who know each other'" Marie parroted Harris' words. Marie pressed her palms together willing thoughts to emerge, "Let's say that Paul did not kill LaCroix, but as you say that usually murder is between people who know each other. What if the murderer knows Paul and knew LaCroix?" Marie wondered how she could figure that out. If only she knew what Paul's real name was.

Harris read his wristwatch and cursed. "Marie, I need to go. I'm meeting with the museum's board to give them a full report of our art recovery." He glanced down at the table next to the couch where the envelope rested. "I really wanted to speak with you about that before you read it. Would you be willing to wait? Maybe until this afternoon? Or later this evening, over dinner?" Marie smiled and nodded. The two stood up at the same time, standing awkwardly close.

"Before you go, Don, do you know when they're going to return the artwork to the museum? If Paul is going after that Fabergé box again, it needs to be kept somewhere safe," Marie said. Harris peered down at Marie, contemplating an answer. He took off his glasses, folded them, and then leaned down, softly kissing her. Fireworks soared in her chest, as he pulled away.

"I guess it'll be up to me to keep that box safe until our thief is apprehended," Harris offered. He kissed Marie one more time on her cheek and left. Marie touched her cheek and could feel the heat rise. She picked up the envelope, resisting the urge to look inside, and placed it on her kitchen counter. She would wait until dinner.

She padded into her bedroom, ready to tumble into her bed for a mid-morning nap. Her eye caught her closed laptop. She knew she just needed to leave well enough alone, but she wondered just how Paul knew LaCroix. Could the key to the murder be in where they grew up? She settled at her small desk and booted up the computer. A little search couldn't hurt.

The streetcar driver clanged the bell as the streetcar approached Esplanade and Carrollton, terminating across from the base of a removed Confederate monument. Paul pulled his ridiculous blue blockers in place and pulled the black and gold baseball cap's visor lower over his eyes. Brassy blonde hair peaked from underneath the cap. He gently tapped his blonde mustache, as he exited the streetcar with fifteen other tourists.

He managed to keep in the middle of the group as they walked down the sidewalk to the entrance of the New Orleans Museum of Art. He stopped periodically to snap a picture with his phone, pocketing it in an outrageously loud purple Mardi Gras sweatshirt over belted khaki shorts and white tennis shoes and socks. He looked like some Midwestern dad, except under his sweatshirt was a six pack.

As the line moved forward, a woman behind the ticket counter invited the group to sign the register with a broad smile. The woman added that the museum loved to find out where people traveled from who had visited the museum. Paul paid for his ticket and took the pen offered to him, scribbling his new name with a flourish. Picking up a map, he opened it and began to wander through the museum, not really looking at anything. He casually ascended the marble staircase, looking right into the eyes of Marie Antoinette at the landing and turning right. At the top of the stairs he wandered to the Fabergé room, blocked off with yellow tape and a security guard.

"What's going on here? New exhibit going in?" Paul asked the security guard. He peered into the room, around the guard. From a distance he could see a group that included a portly man in a blue pinstriped suit, a Helen Mirren-esque woman in pearls and a blue cardigan, and a frail older woman with a cane, all of whom were surrounding Harris—the man he'd seen in Paris. Harris was walking around the room, gesturing at the corners, speaking softly, trying to convince the small group of something.

Paul leaned back quickly and smiled at the security officer.

Had Harris seen him? He didn't want to draw more attention to himself, and he stepped back further. Before he could turn around, the woman in pearls and blue cardigan, stood before him. "Sir, I understand you have a question about this exhibit," the woman inquired, her white hair falling in a charming bob around her unlined face.

"Uh, yeah, are you getting a new exhibit or something?" Paul asked in his best mid-western pseudo-Southern accent. The woman raised her right eyebrow ever so slightly, but in a flash, she smiled at the man.

"Actually, after some upgrades and renovation, the Milton Fabergé Box and all the other Faberge items will be returned to this space," the woman offered helpfully. Paul frowned slightly, making his lip itch from the fake moustache. Seeing his expression, she continued: "I am so sorry you cannot see the exhibit now. All of us on the board love it when folks from far away visit us; where are you from?"

"I'm from Missouri…" Paul offered lamely. He wracked his brain trying to figure out just where Missouri was. He knew it was somewhere in the middle. "…by way of Nebraska." He added the next part, hoping to end the exchange. The woman pursed her lips.

"My name is Margaret Reed. What's yours?" She extended her hand. Paul took her hand and exchanged glances. She was suspicious.

Pumping her hand, he replied, "My name is Philip le Bel. I better go find my wife," he offered lamely, slipping his hand from her grip and pivoting.

He moved quickly toward the elevators, passing them and then—finding a good vantage point—he turned to look back. Margaret Reed was looking in his direction, her head cocked to one side, when Harris and the others joined her outside the room. She spoke directly to Harris who immediately marched in Paul's direction.

Paul ducked into the pre-Columbian art exhibit, heading behind a large column. He pulled off his sweatshirt, cap, wig and moustache, revealing a white polo shirt with a small name tag and logo for Crescent City Tours. He sported frosted tips on his hair, like a 90's boy band reject. He pulled on his pant leg, pulling out two straight pins and transforming the shorts into cargo pants. Moving quickly into the next exhibit, he found a trash can and disposed of the now useless items. He found a small crowd of Japanese tourists and began speaking with them, offering to snap pictures as Harris rushed through the room.

Paul observed Harris through the camera lens. The portly man toddled over to Harris, pulling Harris' arm and whispering something to him. Harris nodded and sighed. The two exited the room. Paul returned the camera and carefully weaved through the small group, bumping one man and removing his red windbreaker that hung over his camera case. He pulled on the jacket, exited the room, following Harris. Somehow he knew that Harris might lead him straight to the Milton Fabergé Box, if he could keep Harris from discovering him first.

Marie read several newspaper articles, translated from French, about the recent murder at the George V. Some only mentioned that a murder had occurred on the premises of the hotel—a robbery gone wrong. Others interviewed the hotel manager about the security measures at the luxury hotel. Finally, she found the one from the day after it occurred, listing LaCroix—or Scott Cross—and Philip Augustin.

She carefully examined two pictures in the article. Paul's photo could have been a glamour shot. LaCroix's photo looked more like a mug shot. As she peered closely at it, she concluded it indeed was a mugshot.

She typed in the name Scott Cross into the obituaries and was flooded with thousands. She added more details to the search, hoping to reduce the results. She added the date of death and then began to scan the articles, finally landing on one from a small London neighborhood website. The picture wasn't there, but as she read the small headline: "Local businessman dies on holiday to Paris."

Marie clicked on the tiny article and read it. It didn't offer any more information than she already knew, except for a small quotation from a Maureen Lloyd of Balfour Street. Marie imagined a little old lady stooped over her cane, speaking to the reporter. "He was a local boy, lived just around the corner. His mum was sweet, but she died. The boy got in a lot of trouble. He looked kind of like a young Marlon Brando, before he got big, if you know what I mean." Marie knew what the little old lady meant.

She typed into her computer the name of the neighborhood and the street name, looking for a map. She clicked through the links until the street map showed on her screen. She peered down at the map and clicked on the streets next to it, reading the names of businesses. *Kings' Court Lane* caught Marie's eye.

Marie clicked on the street view of Kings' Court Lane. She tapped on the computer, virtually moving from house to house down the street. The small brick town houses crowded together, some with laundry in the front yard. Most of the businesses appeared boarded up in the picture. She was just about to shut off the computer when she raced passed a boarded up building on the site. She moved the mouse back and enlarged the picture: Philip Smith, locksmith.

Marie typed the name in the search engine, this time with the street name. An obituary appeared; she opened the link and read the simple paragraph. "Philp John Smith, formerly of Kings' Court Lane, died peacefully in his sleep on Saturday, October 9, 2004 at St. George's Residential Home in Gravesend, after a lengthy illness. Mr. Smith was preceded in death by his beloved wife, Elizabeth, who he claimed was his queen. He is survived by one son, Paul Smith…" Marie closed the top of the laptop. She'd found his name. She'd found Paul! Now what?

She would call Harris and tell him. She reached for her phone but stopped before dialing. What if he was meeting with the museum's board right now? Instead, she texted him, spending twenty minutes trying to wordsmith what ultimately was a simple sentence: "Paul's real name is Paul Smith of Gravesend." Marie added a hug emoji and hit send, before feeling a little foolish about the emoji. Oh well.

Marie re-opened her laptop. She returned to the small article about Scott LaCroix or Cross. She re-read it and realized that something about the way the article was written, even for a small newspaper, seemed too vague. There was no mention of a wife or children, nor about his business or even about what the authorities had said about his death. She clicked on the email address of the writer and composed an email, sending it on its way.

She found the original article, translated from French. She was surprised that the original article seemed to present more personal information about the man. The article wrote that LaCroix or Cross was "a small time drug dealer from Gravesend." She compared the French paper's reporting to the small newspaper and shook her head.

Marie felt surprised when shortly afterwards an email popped into her inbox from the reporter. The reporter thanked Marie for her email and wondered if Marie might be willing to meet her on a video call in a few minutes. Marie clicked on the link and her screen chirped and her face looked out at her from her screen. Grabbing a rubber band she pulled back her hair, but that only made her look like she had a double chin. The reporter at that moment picked up.

"Hello from Gravesend, Ms. Clyde. Can you hear me and can you see me?" A twenty-something girl with a bright red pixie cut appeared on Marie's screen. She waved to the camera. Marie reflexively waved back.

"I'm here and I hear you, Ms. Todd. Thank you so much for being willing to speak with me. This is really nice." Marie smiled at the woman on the screen. They both nodded and then pixels appeared on the screen.

"You can call me Amanda. You said that you were wondering about my article about the late Mr. Cross or LaCroix, as he called himself." The young woman leaned back in her chair from the screen and drew in a breath.

"Yes, I wanted to know what type of business he was involved in. There was no mention of it in the article," Marie asked and leaned forward. That was a mistake. Her nose loomed large on the small screen so she leaned back. Again, she looked like she had a double chin.

The young woman looked around her and then looked into the screen: "Seriously, you don't know what he did?" Marie nodded. This time Amanda leaned toward her screen making her nose appear gigantic. "Mr. Cross worked with or—rather for—the 'Tate' organization."

"What do they do? What does that mean?" Marie picked up her notebook and started to take notes. She could see the woman swallow nervously. "Is it safe for you to speak with me?"

Amanda threw up her hands. "I'm upstairs at my mum's house. It's safe, I guess." Marie held back a laugh, responding to the woman's theatrics. "You never know who's listening." Marie nodded solemnly.

"Why did you not include that he worked for the Tate Organization in your article?" Marie asked earnestly.

"I'm only supposed to write the facts; that's what my boss Mr. Byrd told me, but what I found out from my sources, is that he worked for Tate for almost twenty years. Tate is a gangster around here. You don't cross him and you don't write about him unless you have facts, an actual quotation and a heavy tea kettle for protection. The police here are working on taking down the organization and there was some talk that maybe Cross was going to snitch and that got him killed." Amanda was rubbing her hands together in excitement. "I just know that I could write a story that would blow this thing wide open and then get hired by the Guardian."

"I wonder what a gangster would want with the Milton Fabergé Box in New Orleans," Marie mused aloud, tapping her pencil on the pad. She looked at the wide-eyed girl on the screen.

"Wait, you know something about his death? What did you say? A Faberge Box?" Now the reporter was scribbling on a small notebook as well. "What do you know about Scott Cross and his death in Paris?"

"I was at that hotel the night he died. I believe that he stole the Milton Fabergé Box from the New Orleans Museum of Art and was in Paris to deliver it to the buyer, along with another man. What would a gangster like Tate want with a Fabergé Box?" Marie asked Amanda. Amanda was busy scribbling.

From off-screen a voice called: "Amanda, dear, do you want to come downstairs and watch the bake-off show? I made some cakes."

"Nah, mum; I'm in the middle of an investigation. Keep my

cake warm," Amanda called back. She smiled sheepishly at Marie. "It's a good show. We like to watch it together and make desserts usually." Amanda picked up her notebook and read it and then looked back at the screen, "What is the Milton Fabergé Box? I can't say what a gangster would want with that, but Tate is involved with a lot of different crimes. Everyone is scared to say anything about him here."

Marie thought about what Amanda told her. She wondered what a gangster would have to do with art theft. That seemed a little too high brow for a neighborhood crime boss, but maybe he had some greater ambition? Maybe LaCroix had double crossed him? "I better let you go watch your show. It was nice speaking with you, Amanda." Marie moved to disconnect the video call.

"Wait, but what do you know? Are you a spy? Are you investigating this crime? Are you Interpol? I could write a follow-up story and blow the lid right off this thing." Amanda spoke excitedly into the screen. Marie smiled at the idea that this girl thought she might be an international spy. Marie decided she didn't need to ruin the mystery.

"I tell you what, Amanda, when I've figured this all out, I'll call you for the exclusive." Amanda's shoulders rose to her ears and she grinned broadly.

"Mum, I'm coming down for my cake! Guess what?" she shouted off the side of the screen. She looked back at Marie, "I could tell you were excited from your email. Thanks, good night." Amanda clicked off the call. Marie laughed, thinking about the girl's exuberance.

Marie closed the top of her laptop. She looked down at her notes, underlining Tate. She wrote in flowery cursive: Marie Clyde, Woman of International Intrigue. She put down her pen and picked up her phone, wondering if Harris had gotten her text.

She found three texts waiting for her. One came from David, asking if she could turn over the phone number for the mysterious Philip le Bel to Lisa and Tina. Another text came from Tina, wondering if Marie could check the grammar on a new publication before the end of the day, complete with six grammatical errors. The third text was a number she didn't recognize. All it said was, "Thanks for letting me stay last night. I know where to find it."

Marie immediately dialed Harris' phone number and it went to voicemail. Marie tried to stay calm on the phone: "Harris, Don, he knows where the box is and he's going to find it. He just texted me. Please call me back. It's Marie."

A text appeared on her phone's screen: "On my way to Lydia Milton's home. Will talk later. Thanks for the name. See you at 5:30 tonight." A little heart appeared on the screen. Marie pressed the phone to her chest.

Chapter 20

Harris spent the better part of the afternoon arguing. The day seemed to start well at the museum. He explained the continuing threat to the Milton Fabergé Box, laying out a plan for its protection at the museum. This had seemed like a good idea until one of the members of the board actually spoke with thief intending to steal the Fabergé Box.

A fury of phone calls resulted. At first, Harris thought the encounter would convince the board about the need for his plan. The group traveled to the basement of the museum to examine the safe and the Fabergé Box only to discover the box missing. Again, the group made furious phone calls. Finally, the museum's director arrived on the scene, informing them that the Box's owner would be keeping it until the Fabergé exhibit was renovated and ready for its return.

As a convoy, the museum board traveled to Uptown New Orleans, turning from St. Charles Avenue down oak- lined State Street, stopping in front of a slate-colored grand Victorian-era mansion, with a large welcoming porch framed with gothic columns. The board and Harris gathered on the porch and rang the bell. Harris tried not to press his face against the double-leaded glass front doors. A petit brown-haired woman in a simple black dress opened the door and welcomed them inside.

The woman ushered the group into an elegantly decorated double parlor. Above the marble mantle, Harris recognized a Matisse. On another wall, hung what Harris suspected was a Kandinsky. Members of the group spread across the room and admired and finally sat on the surprisingly comfortable white silk couches.

"Oh my goodness, oh my goodness, what a treat!" said Mrs. Milton. "What is the board of the museum doing here? Please let me get you all tea. Louise, would you please bring the sandwiches?" Lydia Milton stood in the center of the room, surprising her guests. Immediately, members of the group hopped up and embraced the woman. Harris hung back and watched the exchanges. In the corner, one of Mrs. Milton's guards, a man Harris recognized as only Hank appeared, holding his fingers laced in front of him as if he was praying. He, too, watched the group and frowned.

Three other women all wearing the same black dress entered the room with three silver trays piled with sandwiches, drinks, napkins and utensils. The group descended on the trays like vultures. Soon the group was laughing and Mrs. Milton was laughing. They scattered to the different couches and began their small feast. Every minute, the thief was moving closer. Harris felt impatient, but he knew he must wait.

A fourth woman entered the room with a silver teapot, pouring and interacting. She offered a cup to Harris, but he refused. He crossed his arms and could suddenly feel a cold stare from the man in the corner. Harris unfolded his arms and the man stopped. Harris looked as the large man received a cup of tea and silently thanked the server, raising the cup to Harris.

"Oh, Mr. Harris, please join us. You are so serious all the time. Please sit, enjoy my hospitality. You and I can speak after the board leaves." Mrs. Milton said from her perch on the end of one of the couches. Harris tried to contain himself and gave a stiff smile. One of the servers approached him with a sandwich on a plate which he made a show of receiving it and taking a bite.

Harris wondered why Marie had called. The woman had a way of getting into trouble. She also had a way of figuring thing out. He smiled thinking about her.

"So glad you like the sandwich," a voice spoke right next to Harris' ear. He turned suddenly and found himself staring into the middle of an enormous muscled chest. Harris looked up at Hank. He'd met him a little over a week ago with Mrs. Milton. He looked like a rhinoceros stuffed into an expensive suit.

The rhinoceros named Hank smiled down at Harris and patted him on the back. It felt more like being smacked with a frying pan. Harris let out a cough. What was someone like Mrs. Milton doing with muscle like this guy?

Hank waved over a server and asked for a water for Harris. A server immediately appeared with a crystal glass and handed it to Hank who gently handed it to Harris. Harris sipped the water and examined the giant over the rim of the glass. "So, Hank, what do you do for Mrs. Milton?" The giant's face softened.

"She's like a mother to me. Mrs. Milton might not look it, but she's a tough lady, but kind. We met about twenty years ago. I was headed down a dangerous path and she saved me," Hank answered and crossed his arms. Harris was intrigued at the answer. The man pulled a white handkerchief from his back pocket and dabbed his eyes.

Harris looked away. Hank cleared his throat. Harris again looked at the man, but now his expression was blank. Harris looked back at the board members, chattering sweetly. Harris still felt like he wanted to stomp his foot and demand that Mrs. Milton listen to him right now. He could hear the group offering weak explanations why Mrs. Milton should keep the Fabergé Box at the museum. She deftly changed the subject.

Finally, two members of the group moved toward the front door. They offered their thanks and hugged Mrs. Milton. Another two followed. Mr. Drummond stopped at the door and looked sternly at Mrs. Milton: "We really think you need to listen to what Mr. Harris has to say. I know that the Milton Fabergé Box belongs to your family, but please consider keeping it safely locked away at the museum." He shook Mrs. Milton's hand and exited. Mrs. Milton shut the door behind the group and turned to Harris.

Mrs. Milton's heels clicked on the glossy wood floors as she approached Harris in the double parlor. She sat on the white silk couch and looked up at Mr. Harris, leaning back on the couch. She motioned for him to sit across from her and he perched on the other couch.

"Mr. Harris, you have waited so patiently. Why don't you convince me why I should turn over the Milton Fabergé Box to you rather than wait until the exhibit can re-open?" She smiled sweetly at Harris, but he had the distinct impression that she was grinding her teeth. He felt a massive shadow behind him on the couch. He looked over his shoulder at Hank and then back at Mrs. Milton.

He glanced down at his watch. It was already four. He needed to hurry to get the box safely away from this house and make it in time for dinner with Marie.

Paul leaned against an oak tree across the street from a slate-colored Victorian mansion. Under its shade, he appeared to any passerby as a runner, stretching. He knelt down, appearing to tie his shoelaces. He watched as a small party stopped at the large double doors and thanked the host. He recognized one of the women exiting as the one he'd met earlier. The large glass door shut behind the group as they made their way to their cars.

He could see a little bit of movement through the large picture window. If he squinted, he could just make out the outline of who he assumed was that Harris fellow. The other two figures were not as clear, but one appeared enormous. He watched what appeared to be an animated conversation.

He scanned the outside of the house. The house was huge, two stories. White shutters framed large windows. The upstairs sported a small balcony that overlooked the street and another balcony that overlooked the house next door. Bushes and lush vegetation surrounded the house, offering excellent hiding spots. Paul smiled.

He gazed back at the picture window. The room was now empty. He wondered where the group had gone. He assumed they must have gone to the location of the Fabergé box in the house. He jogged a few feet down the street, hoping to look through another window and get a different angle. He crossed the street and found another spot, catching a glimpse through the window of the three, walking up a huge staircase. So, the box was upstairs?

He walked closer to the house. He stopped when he noticed a small black box near the gutter. He recognized a camera, even one as well hidden as this one. He stepped back again and pressed himself against another oak tree. He would need to be careful and he would have to wait until Harris left. He decided he would jog around the block and climb the back fence.

The house directly behind the mansion was a much simpler double shotgun-type house. He walked down the alleyway along the smaller house to a high wooden gate and climbed to the top of it. Behind the gate was a small patio and garden. A large oak leaned over the brick wall, separating the patio from the mansion's backyard. He quickly shot across the space and climbed into the tree. He could see the back of the house now.

A small pool and two-story pool house stood between him and the back porch of the mansion. He watched as two women in black dresses opened the back door and carried out black garbage bags. The two women chatted animatedly as they tossed the trash into cans hidden along the side of the house. He looked at the second floor of the house in which a row of casement windows overlooked the pool.

As if on cue, one of the windows opened and Harris looked out across the yard. Paul felt Harris' eyes upon him. Harris stared into the tree. Paul pressed himself against the branch, hoping nothing was visible. Harris turned back toward the room and the window closed. Paul knew exactly where the box was now. He looked down at his watch. He just needed to wait until dark, surely Harris would leave soon.

Harris pulled the casement window closed and turned toward Hank and Mrs. Milton. The two stood at the doorway of the room, waiting for Harris' response. "I don't like this. The box is not secure in this room." Harris waved toward the row of windows, casting long shadows across the Persian rug.

The Milton Fabergé Box was perched at the center of a marble-topped vanity across from an antique canopied bed. On both sides of the bed were matching marble-top bedside tables. The room was completely devoid of personal effects except one silver-framed photograph of a little girl in a smocked dress on a nightstand. The room looked like a picture from *Southern*

Homes, but it would not be a suitable spot for the Milton Fabergé Box.

"Oh, Mr. Harris, don't be so dramatic. This is where the box belongs. It's a girl's jewelry box." Mrs. Milton leaned her head to the side as she examined Harris. He felt like a child demanding a second ice cream from his doting aunt.

"Please, Mrs. Milton, I have reliable *intel* that the man who attempted to steal this box before and is involved in the murder of one of his associates is here in New Orleans. I believe he will come for this box again. He could be dangerous." Harris pleaded with the woman. Mrs. Milton slowly turned her head to Hank. She pressed her lips together. They communicated something to each other through their expressions, but Harris could not determine what.

"You really think that criminal is coming here?" Mrs. Milton asked, stepping into the room. She wandered to the vanity and appraised her reflection. Her hand reached down and stroked the top of the Milton Fabergé Box. She reached her hand out behind her and Hank gently took her hand and squeezed it. She glanced up at Hank and nodded. "Tell me, Mr. Harris, how did you come about this *intel*? Does anyone else know this? Have you spoken to the police?"

"My source is very reliable. In fact, they were able to assist me in returning the box. I haven't had a chance to speak with the police, but this is probably not their highest priority at the moment," Harris answered. Something nagged in him about the way Mrs. Milton asked the questions.

"Do you believe that he's coming tonight? Our thief?" Mrs. Milton asked. Her tone almost reminded him of someone becoming excited about putting together a dinner party.

"Yes, I believe so. Why don't you let me take it to the museum?" Harris offered. He walked over to Mrs. Milton. She looked at him through the reflection and smiled.

"Why don't you stay here and watch it?" Mrs. Milton asked. She ran her fingers through her hair and pulled some stray eyebrow. She swung around and faced Harris. "This could be your only opportunity to catch him in the act. Wouldn't that be best? Yes, that's what you will do. Let's go downstairs and have a little supper before you set yourself up for the night?" Mrs. Milton exited the room, Hank followed her. Harris' shoulders slumped.

Harris chased behind the two as they quickly descended the front staircase. Harris looked down at his watch. It was already 5:45. He was late for his date with Marie. He was never late for anything.

"Please, I'm begging you, Mrs. Milton. This is dangerous. This man is desperate." Harris ran behind Mrs. Milton.

She lifted one palm, almost like she was waving, "Mr. Harris, I have every faith you will know how to deal with this criminal, this Mr. Smith." Harris followed the two down the stairs and immediately into the dining room. The table was set out with three place settings. Harris sighed.

"Oh look, it's already prepared for us. Please join us, Mr. Harris," Mrs. Milton spoke sweetly.

Marie's alarm went off at 5 p.m. She turned off the alarm. She pushed herself off her bed and began to get ready for her date with Harris.

As she brushed her teeth and then applied lipstick, she looked down at her phone. Strange, no message from Harris. She wondered what they would do tonight. Where would they go to eat? Marie's stomach grumbled with anticipation of something delicious.

She felt so excited. She couldn't wait to tell Harris what she'd learned about LaCroix and the Tate Organization. She was still tickled thinking about Amanda Todd thinking she was a spy. Harris would think that was funny too.

The time flew quickly. At 5:29 she still hadn't hear anything from Harris. That seemed unusual. She decided to pop open her laptop, maybe watch a few *YouTube* videos. He must be running late. As the browser popped up, she scanned through her search history and clicked on the Red Milton Fabergé Box.

For the next few minutes, she read through the museum's description of the box. The charming history of the box and its current owners. She thought about holding the box in her hands and remembered the soft scent of lavender when she'd opened it. How amazing that it still retained the scent from probably decades before. Was that even possible?

Marie looked at the screen of her phone. It was now 5:50. A message from Harris appeared. It read: "I'm still at the Milton house," and a frown-faced emoji. Marie stood up from the desk and stretched.

She typed a message to Harris: "I will head there and wait for you. Give me the address." The three little dots appeared and the address popped up. Marie knew the neighborhood. She checked her reflection in the mirror, gathered her purse, phone and keys, then she left.

Harris typed the address into his phone and put the phone in his pocket. One of the servers began to ladle soup into bowls at each place. The scent was amazing. Was it gumbo?

Mrs. Milton stood behind her chair. Hank stood behind his chair to Mrs. Milton's right. They waited for Harris to enter the dining room. When she nodded, the three sat down at the table.

"I noticed you texting, Mr. Harris. Is everything all right?" Mrs. Milton inquired. One of the servers poured wine into her crystal goblet. Mrs. Milton lifted the glass and sipped. Harris noticed that his glass had been filled as well.

"I have a date this evening. I wanted to let her know that I would be running late. She's heading this way," Harris lamely answered. Hank lifted his wine glass in a fake toast to Harris. Harris felt heat rise in his cheeks.

"Oh, how lovely. Is it that sweet Marie Clyde girl?" Mrs. Milton took a careful bite of her soup. Harris was surprised. What did Mrs. Milton know about Marie or his personal life for that matter? As if sensing his discomfort, she added: "I read your report to the board that Ms. Clyde helped you. Mr. Drummond shared it with me. I just deduced." Harris nodded at her answer.

Still something felt unsettling about the situation. Everyone was entirely too calm. Something nagged at Harris. What was it that Mrs. Milton had said earlier? Harris tasted the gumbo. It was amazing, but he had to remember what she'd said. His phone dinged and without thinking, he pulled the phone out to read the message from Marie saying she was outside. He smiled and then he read the earlier message.

"Is she here already? Louise, please go out and invite Ms. Clyde in to join us. I want to talk to her. She knew my daughter in high school." Mrs. Milton smiled broadly at Harris. Louise, the server moved quickly to the front doors.

Harris almost shot out of his seat. "No, please don't bring her in here!" Both Mrs. Milton and Hank stared at Harris with confused expressions. Harris sat back down. "I don't want us to be an imposition on you, Mrs. Milton." Mrs. Milton smiled again and sipped her wine. Hank chortled.

Marie entered the dining room nervously. She looked beautiful in her blue dress. "Thank you so much for inviting me in, Mrs. Milton. You are too kind." A server placed another setting at the table, across from Harris, next to Hank. Marie took her place and smiled at Harris. He looked pale.

"I think I should go check on the box." Harris stood up. Hank stood up as well. Harris stared at Marie, trying to communicate something with his eyes.

"If you think that is best, Mr. Harris. I say go right ahead. Hank, please accompany him." Mrs. Milton spoke like a queen, "Now, Marie, you must tell me all about yourself. I understand from the museum's board that you had quite an adventure with Mr. Harris." Harris and Hank exited the room, with Harris looking over his shoulder at Marie.

Harris took two stairs at a time, with Hank close on his heels. When they reached the first landing, Harris stopped in an attempt to have Hank go ahead of him, but the giant said "After you, Mr. Harris. You know the way." Harris topped the stairs and looked around. Maybe he could grab a weapon or find a way out of the house, but how could he tell Marie?

As he approached the bedroom with the Milton Fabergé Box, he noticed a shadow under the door. He paused for a moment and then rushed through the door. No one was there. Hank stood directly behind Harris, "Did you see something?"

Harris turned and faced the mountain of a man, looking his straight in the eye. "I thought I saw a shadow in here, but nothing seems to be disturbed." Both men scanned the room. The red box sat perched in its spot on the vanity. The bed, neatly made, appeared untouched. Only a single lamp on the nightstand illuminated the room. "I guess we should go back downstairs and finish dinner."

Harris lunged to the left of the man, but Hank slugged Harris in the stomach. Harris released a weak groan and collapsed to the floor. He looked up at the larger man. "I can't let you leave now, Mr. Harris, not when Mrs. Milton is so close." The huge man balled his hands into fists. Harris' eyes widened.

"Why are you doing this?" Harris asked as Hank drew back

his fist to strike. Hank paused for a moment and Harris thought for a moment that he would answer but the fist swooped down, striking Harris in the face, knocking him out.

Marie watched Harris leave and she had the distinct impression that he was in danger, but she didn't know why. When she entered the dining room, Harris' expression changed from awe to fear. Or at least she thought it was fear.

"How was your trip to Paris, Ms. Clyde? Please tell me everything," Mrs. Milton interrupted her thoughts. Marie nodded at the kind older woman and sipped her wine. "It appears you lucked out with the weather, only one rainy day."

"It was really exciting, Mrs. Milton. I got to see all the sights and I helped figure out where the stolen artwork was." Mrs. Milton smiled at Marie and took a bite of her gumbo. "The weather really did cooperate. I went to the Eiffel Tower probably every day and ate a ton of macaroons." Both women laughed.

"Not that one ever needs an excuse, but why did you go to Paris? Were you investigating this thief as well?" Mrs. Milton inquired. She unconsciously touched the ruby pin on her lapel.

"I guess I was inspired to go there after I figured out that was where he was headed." Marie thought about her standing at the counter at the Ritz Carlton. Would anyone believe that she'd gotten there because of Peaceful Lavender Mint shampoo? She could do a weird commercial for that shampoo company someday. Marie inhaled over her soup, noticing its scent. She noticed another familiar scent. "Is that lavender?"

"My, what a good nose you have. Guilty as charged, I use a lavender-scented hand cream. I cannot get enough of it." Mrs. Milton laughed. "My sweet Rose got it for me a few years ago, when she started getting better, and I could never change it now.

If the store stops selling it, I'll burn the place down!" Mrs. Milton banged the table dramatically. Marie had the distinct impression that Mrs. Milton was not kidding. "So, how did you find the Milton Fabergé Box?"

"Actually, the thief…" Marie began to tell her story.

"Paul Smith?" Mrs. Milton offered helpfully.

"Yes, Paul Smith handed me the box at the George V. He was covered…" She stopped talking. Marie thought back to the evening at the George V. She remembered her horror at seeing the blood on Paul. She remembered slipping into the bathroom and examining the box, inhaling its scent. Marie grew quiet. Mrs. Milton stared intensely at Marie.

"You must have been terribly shocked. After all, he'd just killed his old friend from Gravesend. How frightening," Mrs. Milton spoke sweetly to Marie, but the hair on Marie's arm stood straight up. She wondered if Mrs. Milton could see her reaction. Mrs. Milton signaled the server to bring out the next course, again her hand rubbed the pin on her lapel.

"Yes, it was scary… This gumbo is delicious…Mrs. Milton, I noticed your pin. It's really lovely." Marie complimented the woman, hoping to distract the older woman. Two servers appeared and replaced the bowls with the main dish, a delicious Trout Almondine with asparagus. Marie looked down at her plate. Her appetite left her and it wasn't because of the dish.

"Oh this? This was Rose's broach. Some young man in London gave it to her when she went on a semester abroad. She said the color reminded her of our Fabergé Box and her sweet grandmother. Rose and her grandmother were very alike, sweet but naïve. Thankfully, for her grandmother—my mother in law—she met a nice man, Mr. Milton. Not so for my poor Rose…" Mrs. Milton drifted off. Marie followed her gaze to the staircase. Marie wondered what was taking Harris so long. Mrs.

Milton kept talking, "This is the only item Rose didn't sell to buy drugs over the last twenty years. The reason I loaned the Milton Fabergé Box to the New Orleans Museum of Art was because I couldn't trust Rose not to sell it. But this she held onto, even keeping the fake leather box it came in. Can you imagine?" Mrs. Milton took off the broach and held it up to the light, twirling it. "A gift from a criminal. Just a thief pretending to be a king."

Mrs. Milton placed the broach on the table and sipped her wine. She carefully re-pinned it to her lapel. Marie considered what Mrs. Milton said and replayed it in her mind. Marie looked again at the staircase. Piece by piece started to fall into place. Mrs. Milton silently motioned to the server who immediately handed Mrs. Milton a small black purse.

"Mrs. Milton, how did you know the thief's name? How did you know..." Marie asked in a whisper, realizing her mistake in speaking. Mrs. Milton leaned over her plate.

"What did you say, my dear?" Mrs. Milton asked sweetly, sounding like a doting grandmother or the witch in *Hansel and Gretel*.

"I was wondering how your family came to have that fabulous Fabergé box." Marie picked up her glass and sipped, smiling brightly.

"Oh that's an interesting story, Marie. My late husband's mother was a bit of a free spirit, a lot like my Rose. As a young woman, before World War II, she traveled in Europe with a tutor for a summer and met a dashing young count, or whom she thought was a count. He turned out to be nothing but a scoundrel. He pretended to be the count of a small European kingdom that doesn't exist anymore. He wined and dined her and bought her the Milton Fabergé Box. Her father got wind of the situation, and promptly sent a representative to escort her back to the United States. She initially refused, insisting that she was going to marry the pretender, but the real count died suddenly. So, heartbroken, believing her lover to be dead, Mrs. George Milton returned home with only a token from her former lover. Of course, between you and me, I think she might have come home with more than a Fabergé Box. I always thought there was a little bit of scoundrel in my George." Mrs. Milton winked. Marie realized that Mrs. Milton must have told this story a thousand times and perfected it.

"What a romantic story!" Marie clapped and Mrs. Milton lifted her wine glass in a mock toast. The two laughed.

"It is a romantic story. My mother-in-law was like that, so was my Rose. Always being taken in by some criminal. You need to tell me, how did you find that thief? You are a regular detective," Mrs. Milton asked curiously.

Marie looked over her shoulder towards the stair. Was that a thud? "Strangely enough, I first found him through his shampoo. The scent was very distinctive…" Marie realized why the lavender scent was so familiar. The box smelled like lavender, not from some time long ago, but because Mrs. Milton had touched and handled the box on the night of LaCroix's murder. The two women looked at each other. Mrs. Milton stared icily at Marie. Marie instinctively rubbed her arms, willing the hair to stop standing on end and warm her.

"Louise, why don't you and Natalie and Thea head home?" Mrs. Milton leaned her head back on her chair.

"No dessert tonight, Madame? Natalie made crème brulée." Louise pressed her hands together hoping to entice Mrs. Milton. Mrs. Milton scrunched her nose and shook her head.

"No, I don't think so. Not tonight. Hank and I will clean everything up and we'll see you tomorrow." Mrs. Milton dismissed the smiling woman. Marie watched the woman leave and drew in a deep breath. Marie looked down at her plate, moving her fork around, hoping that Mrs. Milton had not noticed.

"This just looks delicious. I wish that Mr. Harris would come downstairs and try it before it gets cold. It's really a shame to let crème brulée go to waste. Too bad really," Marie spoke, trying to push the anxiety from her voice. She peered up from the plate and Mrs. Milton looked across the table at Marie. She was not smiling. Mrs. Milton leaned back in her chair and dropped her hands to her lap.

"Marie, I think that you're a very smart woman, but you wear your emotions across your face. I want you to know that I think that's a sign of good character. Unfortunately for you, I have bad character." Mrs. Milton lifted her right hand and placed it on the table. She held a small pearl-handled revolver.

"What are you doing? Why do you have a gun?" Marie asked incredulously. She swallowed hard, trying to stay calm. "Please, Mrs. Milton, why are you doing this?"

Mrs. Milton pushed back her chair and stood, pointing the gun at the middle of Marie's chest. She held the gun with both hands and signaled for Marie to get up. Carefully Marie pushed back from the table and stood. "Move!" Mrs. Milton commanded and she motioned the gun in the direction of the staircase. Marie stepped backward, holding her hands up. "Turn around and walk up the stairs, slowly."

Marie listened to hear if anyone else was in the house. She could hear the alarm beep on the kitchen door, signaling that someone had left. She paused at the bottom of the grand staircase and looked up. The upstairs was dark, like the opening of a lion's jaws.

"I said, go up the stairs!" Mrs. Milton demanded. Marie felt the muzzle of the gun in the middle of her back. Marie nodded and took a step. Fear gripped Marie. She felt like she would freeze in place, but she lifted her foot on the next stair. "You don't have to go that slow." Again Marie felt the muzzle on her back.

"Please, Mrs. Milton, please tell me why you're doing this? Why? What have I done to you?" Marie asked pleadingly. The two made it to the first landing and Marie turned slightly to see Mrs. Milton's face. Mrs. Milton pursed her lips and squinted her eyes at Marie. She motioned with the gun. At the top of the second set of stairs, Marie stopped and again turned back toward Mrs. Milton.

"Where now?" Marie asked, her voice shaking.

"Down this hall to Rose's room," she barked at Marie.

"Which one is Rose's room?" Marie asked. She gestured at the several doors.

"Move it," growled Mrs. Milton. She jabbed the gun into Marie's back and Marie stumbled forward.

Marie walked down the long hallway. All the doors were shut and dark except for one. She could see a light under the door. When she reached the end of the hallway, Marie knocked and opened the door. To her surprise, she saw Harris sitting in a chair with his hands behind him. His head lagged to one side.

Marie instinctively ran to him and checked the growing red bump on his head. Harris let out a small groan. Marie was momentarily relieved and then instantly furious, "What did you do to him? Why are you doing this? He needs help!" Before Marie could stop herself, she ran toward Mrs. Milton, only stopping when the gun aimed at Marie's forehead.

"Get back!" Mrs. Milton barked at Marie. Marie raised her hands again and stepped backwards.

Hank emerged from a darkened corner of the room holding another chair and more rope. The man moved closer and closer to Marie, placing the chair next to Harris. At first, he pointed to the chair for Marie to sit down. She shook her head and he grabbed and squeezed her shoulder. "Ow, you're hurting me! Okay, okay." She quickly complied and sat. He then preceded to tie her hands behind her back. "Please, Mrs. Milton, let us go. Harris and I can just walk out of here and forget whatever it is you think we know. I don't know anything."

Mrs. Milton leaned against the vanity as she spoke: "Marie, I know that you're a smart woman. I truly am sorry that you and your beau had to come between me and my revenge. If it's any consolation to you, Hank and I will ensure that you and Mr. Harris are hailed as heroic young folks trying to protect a little old lady from a murderous thief. Unfortunately, that means that you two will die, but I promise to pray about it every week and ask God for forgiveness, but…"

"But, there's no 'but' if you're going to kill me and Don. Why would you do that? You at least owe me that information." Marie needed to keep the woman talking. Perhaps a plan would emerge. Perhaps Harris would awaken and kick butt. She nudged him lightly with her elbow.

"I told you—revenge?" Mrs. Milton answered and wrinkled her brow in confusion. She pointed the gun at Harris. His head lolled to one side.

"Wait, that's not explaining anything. What do you mean 'revenge'? For what? And why? And against who?" Marie could throw as many questions as she could think of. *At a time like this, being a bore had its advantages*, Marie thought.

"Revenge for my Rose!" Mrs. Milton shouted at Marie. "That bastard and his friend killed my daughter!" Marie leaned back in her chair. Hank leaned away from Mrs. Milton. She swung the gun wildly in the air and a bullet hit the ceiling of the room. Everyone grew quiet for a moment.

"Paul, the thief, killed Rose? I thought she died of liver failure," Marie spoke softly.

Mrs. Milton focused on Marie and shook her head, "You don't understand. Rose never used a drug in her life until she went to London. When she went to London, she met a boy and his friend. She liked him. She loved him. He, in turn, bought her this trinket." Mrs. Milton gripped the broach on her lapel, "and then she started using drugs with his friend. He just left her. She barely finished that semester of school and she came home high. It took her 18 years to finally quit but the damage was done. For two years, I held my baby while she withered away. Now, the only thing I have left is making them pay for killing my daughter."

Marie digested what the woman said, "How did you find them? How did you know they were from Gravesend?"

"The box for her broach had the name of a jeweler in Gravesend. I remembered my daughter telling me that he got it for her from down the street from his house. It didn't take much to find that dump." Mrs. Milton laughed mirthlessly. "Then I have my dear Hank here. He is very persuasive and has many friends. Through his connections I found Mr. LaCroix rather easily. That piece of work never got that far from home. All I needed was to dangle some cash in front of his boss and off Mr. LaCroix went, like a lap dog. That fool thought he was getting a payday, wanted to cut out his boss, a gangster. I imagine Mr. Tate would probably have gotten around to Mr. LaCroix eventually. Now, Mr. Smith worked a lot harder at not being found, but I figured it out. Such delusions of grandeur, pretending to be royalty. I saw pictures of Kings' Court Lane. That place is the farthest place from royalty. Again I only need to dangle some cash. We were supposed to get them both in Paris." Mrs. Milton and Hank exchanged a knowing glance.

Marie felt Harris shift next to her; he brushed his hand against hers.

"So, you shot LaCroix at the George V, but you left the box there. Why?" Marie put the pieces together and Mrs. Milton nodded.

"How did you know I was there?" Mrs. Milton asked. She leaned forward curiously. She crossed her arms with the gun dangling on her side.

"The box smelled like your lavender lotion; you touched the box. You also knew that Paul had handed me the box after he supposedly killed LaCroix," Marie answered. Mrs. Milton looked to the ceiling and shrugged. Hank nodded. Marie now realized that Hank had been following her, though she wondered how she hadn't ever see him. How could she have missed him?

"I thought for sure that he would take the box, make contact, and I'd kill him then, but he gave you the box. I knew that I'd framed him for LaCroix's murder. I needed to box him in, if you will," The woman laughed at her joke. Hank rolled his eyes and Marie nodded.

"So, now what? What's your big plan? You're going to kill Harris and me. Then you're going to lure Paul here, shoot him, and then call the police?" Marie asked. Actually, the woman's plan sounded pretty airtight. That wasn't good. "How are you going to explain two people being tied up in here? Those bruises on Harris?"

"Simple, Hank will untie you and arrange you on the floor. No one will notice the bruises. Believe me, it will work." Mrs. Milton nodded confidently.

"How will you explain the gunshot wounds?" Marie shot back. She immediately regretted challenging a woman with a gun. Mrs. Milton and Hank looked at each other. Both looked confused. "All the gunshot wounds will come from the same gun? I think that someone would think that very suspicious. You're also going to make a heck of mess on this carpet!"

Finally, an idea came to Marie; she cocked her head to one side as if listening. "What was that?" Marie whispered. "Someone else is here, we're saved!" Marie rocked in her chair, noticing that the ropes became looser and looser. Marie acted as if she was about to scream when Hank crossed the room and covered Marie's mouth with his meaty hand. He growled into her ear, "Not a word!"

Mrs. Milton swung around to look behind her, cracking the door to the darkened hallway open. She stood straight up in surprise as if someone was there. Marie noticed that her hands were free. Harris must have untied them. She felt him press one finger on her wrist, then two and then a third. Marie swung her fist to the front of Hank's pants, making contact. She also bit down on his hand. At the same time, Harris threw his chair at Mrs. Milton, knocking her to the ground. He then swung the chair back at Hank, cracking him square in the face. Hank sunk to the floor, curling into the fetal position, holding his stomach and his nose. Hank squeaked and coughed.

Harris took the gun from Mrs. Milton and found a phone in Hank's jacket pocket. He dialed 911, speaking to the operator. In moments, they heard the sirens turning from St. Charles Avenue on their way. Harris and Marie looked down at the two when they heard a light tap on the door.

Harris opened the door. Paul leaned against the door jamb with his arms crossed. He stepped silently into the room and scanned it. Paul leaned over Mrs. Milton, reaching down, checking her pulse. He wandered over to Hank and pushed him to his side. Straightening up, he scratched his head and reached into his back pocket, handing Harris a cellphone. He crossed the room and pulled at a spot on the wall. He showed it to Harris. It was a camera. He handed it to Harris as well.

"Were you out there the whole time?" Harris asked incredulously. Paul shrugged. "That behemoth cleaned my clock. Were you ever going to help?" Harris scowled at Paul.

"It looked like you were handling it. You know, I could have grabbed the box anytime, but I waited because I knew it was a setup, but I didn't know why. So, I came in, put in my camera and waited," Paul explained.

"You thought that was handling it? You have a much higher opinion of my abilities than I do." Harris sounded shrill, but Marie patted him on his back. She took his hand in hers and squeezed it.

"I guess I do. You found me, didn't you?" Paul replied. He glanced down at Marie and Harris' interwoven fingers. A shadow crossed Paul's face.

The three stood silently in the room. Paul's eyes took in every corner of the room. He focused on the silver-framed picture of a young Rosa Milton. He picked up the frame and touched the photograph. "All this because of Rose. I remember her. She looked like a model, but she didn't know it or she didn't believe it. I remember buying her that broach. I wanted to impress her, and she broke my heart. That last night I saw her, she kissed Cross and I left. I didn't know about the drugs. Maybe I didn't want to know about it. I just thought she'd dropped me. I never knew what happened to her. I guess I thought she would be married to some stockbroker with three kids in a carpool by now. I didn't know she would still keep the broach. I didn't realize that she would still think about me. I didn't know." Paul stroked the picture and placed it on the nightstand. Harris and Marie listened.

Paul walked to the vanity and picked up the Milton Fabergé

Box. He turned it over in his hands. "I don't suppose I could take it now?" Paul asked Harris and Marie. Both shook their heads no. He placed the box on the table. Paul smiled at Harris and Marie. Paul reached a hand to Marie and pulled her into a quick embrace and kissed her cheek.

"Hey!" Harris protested. Paul released Marie from his embrace. They could hear the wailing of police sirens. Paul and Harris looked each other up and down. A crooked smile crossed Harris' face and he motioned to the doorway. They heard the banging from the front door, Paul waved and ran from the room.

"Do you think that we'll ever see him again?" asked Marie.

"I'd count on it," Harris answered, hugging Marie.

"Police, we're coming in!" someone announced from downstairs. Marie and Harris ran to the staircase and looked down at the approaching officers. Both sagged with relief.

"We're upstairs! Please hurry!" Marie shouted to the officer. Harris crumpled to the ground, rubbing the side of his head. Marie sat next to him, gingerly touching his face. She kissed him softly.

"You're going to be just fine. We're going to be fine," Marie reassured him, as the officer came closer.

Chapter 21

The airport terminal felt hollow and cold. A man in a grey uniform pushed a polisher across the floor while the flight crews in matching blue and white silently pulled their carry-ons. From his spot, Paul watched as the small plane parked at the gate. Paul looked down at his phone, checking the time.

The announcement to board the flight to Mexico City echoed in the emptiness. Paul examined the other passengers. Some were half asleep. One man chatted in Spanish on his cellphone. Another typed furiously on a laptop. He showed his ticket to the gate agent and smiled at the woman.

He looked back at the terminal, checking. No police hurried through the cavernous hallway toward the plane. He boarded the plane and found his seat.

Once seated, Paul stretched his legs across the footrest and reclined his seat. He pushed his head into the plush leather. The flight attendant handed Paul a champagne flute and cloth napkin. He winked at her. Sighing, he sipped his drink.

He put his drink down on the tray table and reached into his pocket. He pulled the ruby broach from his pocket, gripping it tightly in his hand. He opened his palm and examined it, thinking back. He remembered lying next to the sweet girl from America, her head resting on his arm. She kissed him on the cheek and promised never to take the pin off. He put the broach back in his pocket and sipped his champagne.

The captain announced that the flight would be taking off shortly and requested passengers put their seats in their upright positions and fasten their seat belts. Paul adjusted his seat and reached over to the seat next to him. He unzipped the padded black computer satchel and peered inside. He had his small laptop, passport, and toiletries. All were ordinary items. He zipped the bag shut and patted it. The padding he replaced with the five large enveloped, each filled with $20000.

The evening before Paul patiently waited in the tree in the backyard of the Milton house, waiting for a moment to cross the yard unobserved. He focused on what he assumed must be the kitchen door. One woman stepped outside and lit a cigarette. She looked back through the doorway, holding the cigarette away from her body, as she answered someone inside.

She took a quick drag and stubbed out the cigarette on the bottom of her shoe. She then descended the steps and walked to the alley toward the garbage cans. Paul climbed down the tree and shot across the yard and through the door. He ducked immediately to his left in a large walk-in pantry, pulling the door closed behind him. He heard the woman enter and cross the kitchen, talking to the other two women.

He pushed the door slightly to look through the crack. The three women picked up dishes and utensils and left the kitchen. Paul quickly left the closet, found a back stairway and padded up the stairs. On the second floor, he could hear Harris, Mrs. Milton and Hank descending the front staircase. He froze when he heard Mrs. Milton say: "Mr. Harris, I have every faith you will know how to deal with this criminal, Mr. Smith."

Paul pressed against the wall. Mrs. Milton knew his name. The voice on the phone knew his name. He silently padded down the hallway, reaching the bedroom that faced the backyard. He opened the door and saw the Milton Fabergé Box on the desk in the bare room. He pulled the small camera from his pocket, crossed the room and placed it on the wall, angling it toward the center of the room. He checked the phone and the picture was clear.

He left the room and checked the room across the hallway. The room was modern and decorated in beige and white. On one wall hung an oil painting, presumably of the family, a much younger Mrs. Milton, her husband and an infant wearing a bonnet. Paul approached the painting and pulled it from the wall, revealing a safe.

He made quick work opening it. It held four shelves of jewelry, paper files, and a cardboard box filled with almost 100 bulging white envelopes. Next to the box, he noticed a small, leather box. He picked up the familiar item and turned it over in his hand. The corners were now worn and he popped open the box, reading the faded gold script. Rose. It was the box for the broach he'd bought Rose. How was Rose involved in all this?

He closed the box and put it back in the safe. He flipped through the folders and his eyes caught his name. He let out a ragged breath. He took five envelopes from the box. He decided that five would be plenty for his trouble. He shut the safe and returned the portrait to its spot.

He stood next to the door when he heard Hank and Harris walking down the hallway. He waited and heard the door across the hallway open and Harris' grunts. The door closed and Paul opened the door to the bedroom. Harris tried to reason with

Hank, but Paul heard the sound of a fist hitting what Paul assumed was Harris' body.

Paul leaned against the wall and listened. The room was quiet, but the enormous man did not exit. He should leave. *Run*, he thought to himself. He pressed his eyes closed. He walked to the top of the staircase, looking down to the first floor and he heard Marie speaking with Mrs. Milton. How did she get there?

He jerked back from the staircase. He should take off. He would get caught. He heard Marie at the foot of the staircase. Mrs. Milton barked an order at Marie and pointed a gun. Paul flew down the hallway to the bedroom with the portrait. He closed the door behind and pulled out the phone. A gun shot rang out.

He watched the exchange between Marie and Mrs. Milton in the room. He couldn't run away. He needed to help them. Paul dialed 911 and silently spoke to the operator. He opened the door, stepped in front of the other doorway, ready to enter. He would not run away. The door opened and Paul and Mrs. Milton stood face to face. Shock crossed her face and she stumbled back into the room in time for a chair to strike her.

"Excuse me, Mr. Hapsburg, but I will have to ask that you stow your computer. Would you like me to place it in overhead compartment?" The elegant woman in blue and white offered sweetly. Paul nodded and gently handed her the bag. She opened the compartment above her head and stored it.

"Mr. Hapsburg, may I get you another drink?" She smiled expectantly at Paul.

"I'd love another drink." Paul lifted his glass to the woman and she immediately produced a bottle and poured. "And please, call me Philip."

Over the next twenty-four hours, Marie and Harris answered hundreds of questions from multiple police agencies from several countries. Mrs. Milton and Hank pretended that they'd been attacked, but their pleas fell on deaf ears when Harris played the recording for the authorities. Soon, Lydia Milton began to tell her story, claiming that she must be starting dementia.

A little more investigating revealed Mrs. Milton paid several investigators in her search for Scott Cross and Paul Smith. There was also a hefty payment to a known gangster in Gravesend. Airline tickets and customs showed her traveling to Paris and credit card charges proved she paid for LaCroix's room using the name of Philip Augustus. Finally, ballistics showed that her gun was used to shoot Mr. LaCroix.

When the police finally finished their questioning, it was late in the afternoon. Harris and Marie decided to head to a late lunch. The two drove in silence to a quiet local restaurant called Frankie and Johnnie's. They pulled into the shell and gravel covered parking lot and parked.

A sandwich board chalk board out front announced the specials. Inside, little red and white checked tablecloths covered dozens of tables scattered around a large room and football game highlights played on several big screen televisions. The host greeted them and showed them to a table in a quiet corner, directly beneath a chalkboard menu. Harris immediately ordered a beer and Marie ordered a root beer and onion rings.

Marie pulled out her cellphone and looked through her messages. The first one was from Amanda Todd. The subject line read: Can I get an exclusive? Included in the message was a link to a Reuters' story about an incident involving the Milton Fabergé Box and the arrest of Lydia Milton. The rest were desperate messages from Tina, Lisa and David. The final one asking when Marie would be returning and if she could please, please give them the direct number for Mr. Philip la Bel. Marie just shook her head. "Don, I need to call into work."

Marie stepped outside the restaurant, finding a bench on the front porch. She plopped down and dialed her work number. When the receptionist picked up, Marie asked to speak to David, the boss. David answered with an exasperated tone: "Well it's about time, Ms. Clyde. Why aren't you at work?"

Marie pulled the phone from her ear because David was almost shouting. "It turns out that neither Tina, nor Lisa know how to use our database to research anything. We really need to contact that Mr. LaBelle and the last four reports we sent out last week each had multiple errors. The last few days have been a disaster."

"Gosh, that sounds terrible, David. I wonder what you will do." Marie spoke in a soothing voice like an adult would speak to a baby. "I'd really like to help, but I thought that all 'inessential workers' were on furlough? Aren't I 'inessential'? Surely, Tina and Lisa can figure it all out with that big project they have." Marie controlled her giggles. A woman with a stroller walked down the sidewalk in front of Marie. A small child sat up in the stroller and waved a chubby hand at Marie. She wiggled her fingers back at the baby.

"Uh, well, don't you think that you could come in today?" David asked helplessly. She heard him cover the phone and shout to someone. Marie heard him say: "We need to get all those reports back, check them again before we resubmit them. Why does this take seven people to screw this up when Marie could get it right in one shot?" He cleared his throat and spoke to Marie: "Do you think that you could maybe come in?"

"Are you going to fire me?" Marie asked. Strangely, she didn't care what his answer was either way. David was silent.

"Well, we do have some re-structuring going on, but I, uh…" David hemmed and hawed. Marie shook her head. Certainly her order of onion rings was at the table by now.

"Are you going to pay me if I come in?" Marie asked. Again David blustered and rattled through excuses. Marie just sighed. She cut him off, "I tell you what, let me get back to you."

"What about Mr. le Bel's phone number and contact information? Don't you think that we can get that from you right now?" Marie pressed her lips together, trying not to laugh.

"I will really need to get back to you about that. I believe he's traveling at the moment and I'm not sure when I'll ever see him again," Marie responded cheerfully. She thought about where Paul might be and smiled. Who was he now? *Which monarch*, she wondered. "I better go, David, I'm sure that you will figure this all out, and I'll see you in another week when the furlough is over. Bye!" Marie hung up the phone.

Marie returned to the table, smiling down at Harris. She noticed the red spot on the side of his face. It looked a little swollen. She gently touched it and asked the waitress for some ice. The woman returned with a plastic bag filled with ice and Harris held it to his face.

Marie sat down across from Harris. The two sipped their drinks, just looking at each other. He adjusted the ice on his face and then put down the bag. "So, what did your work want?" Harris picked up a napkin and dried the side of his face.

Marie wrinkled her nose, "Suddenly, it seems that 'boring, old Marie' might be more useful than David, my boss, first realized. They need help and they want the phone number of a certain 14th century monarch. Both of which I declined to offer, at the moment, if ever again. Also, he won't say that he won't fire me." Marie held up both her palms. She waved one dismissively and picked up her drink.

"You don't seem too worried about that?" Harris probed. He sipped his beer. Marie thought for a moment and shook her head.

"I guess I'm not as scared about it anymore. I certainly need a job, but maybe I need to be open to actually pursuing something that enjoy." Marie spoke nonchalantly. Harris looked nervous.

"Marie, did you get a chance to open that envelope?" Marie looked blankly at Harris. This was an abrupt change of subject. What was he talking about? "You know, the envelope that I asked you not to open?"

"Yes, it's sitting on my kitchen counter." Marie nodded. She sipped her Barq's. The waitress dropped the basket of onion rings in front of Marie. Marie rubbed her hands together in delight. She immediately grabbed one and crammed the blazing hot ring in her mouth. "So hot." Marie waved her hand over her mouth and took a gulp of her drink and then let out an enormous burp.

Harris stared at her wide eyed. "Wow, you just, wow." Harris pulled his small notebook from his pocket and scribbled something in it. Marie leaned across the table trying to read his writing upside down.

"What did you write?" Marie asked. She blew on another onion ring and mashed it into her mouth. She chewed carefully as she watched him.

Ignoring her question, he pulled a folded envelope from his other top breast pocket. He unfolded it and handed the envelope to Marie. She cautiously took the envelope from him and turned it over in her hands.

"Do you want me to open this one?" Marie asked. She wiped off her greasy fingers on a scrunched-up napkin in her lap.

"This one is actually different than the other one. I guess go ahead and open this one first and I will tell you what's in the other one." Harris said. He sipped his beer. He carefully picked up one onion ring with his fork and placed it on his plate, slicing it into bite size pieces. Marie tore open the envelope and pulled out a check made out to her from an insurance company. Her mouth dropped open when she saw four zeros behind the number two!

"What's this?" Marie almost shouted. All at once she felt hot and cold. She shot up from her seat. The four other patrons in the restaurant turned to their table. Harris smiled and waved at them.

"That's your half of the finder's fee. You helped me successfully return four pieces of stolen artwork to their rightful or appropriate owner. The insurance company gives a finder's fee based on the percentage of what it might cost to replace the artwork should it never be found." Harris answered calmly. He took a small bite of his onion ring and closed his eyes, savoring the taste.

"It's made out to me? Its mine?" Marie held the check to her chest. She couldn't believe it. She waved the check like a fan, trying to cool down the flush across her face.

"Yes, it' yours to keep or do with it what you will, but I suggest putting it in a bank," Harris answered. He took another bite, chewed and put down his fork, "Marie, this brings me to the other envelope. The one you have at home. I want to offer you a partnership. I want you to work with me and help me find artwork. Would you like to do that? It would mean travel, expensive meals, fancy clothing…" Marie could barely breathe. She was pretty sure he was serious, except for the last few things he said. "Hanging out with me…" he said the last part quietly, looking her straight in the eye. She could see that he wasn't sure how she would respond.

Marie reached her hand across the table and took his hand. "Don, I would love to play detective with you." Harris lifted her hand to his lips and he kissed it.

"Okay, then let me tell you about where we're going next…" He flipped through the pages of his small notebook and began to read aloud his notes while Marie shoved another onion ring in her mouth.

About the Author

 Mary E. Koppel is a New Orleans' girl living on the Mississippi Gulf Coast. A mother, traveler and lover of mystery and romance, Mary is blessed with constant curiosity that has only gotten her into a little bit of trouble. She has written one book of essays, co-authored a book of non-fiction, and has written essays and devotions for a few blogs and publications.

Mary writes the Denise Reed mystery series which includes *Volunteer to Die* and *Hotdog Down*. *Runaway Fabergé* is the first in her Art Detective mysteries.

www.ingramcontent.com/pod-product-compliance
Lightning Source LLC
Chambersburg PA
CBHW020329260626
47156CB00004B/1440